Topics of Conversation

Topics of
Conversation

MIRANDA POPKEY

First published in Great Britain in 2020 by
Serpent's Tail,
an imprint of Profile Books Ltd
29 Cloth Fair
London
ECIA 7JQ
www.serpentstail.com

First published in the United States in 2020 by
Alfred A. Knopf, a division of Penguin Random House, New York

Jacket photograph by Maria Švarbová
Jacket design by Sinem Erkas

10 9 8 7 6 5 4 3 2 1

Printed and bound in Great Britain by
Clays Ltd, Elcograf S.p.A.

A CIP catalogue record for this book is available from the British
Library.

ISBN 978 1 78816 404 7
eISBN 978 1 78283 641 4

This book is for WRM,
and also for Kent Lowell

How to recognize a story?
There is so much experience but
the real outcome tyrannizes over it.

—SYLVIA PLATH,
from a journal entry dated December 28, 1958

Topics of Conversation

Italy, 2000

From the shore, the sea in three pieces like an abstract painting in gentle motion. Closest to the sand, liquid the pale green of a fertile lake. Then a swath of aquamarine, the color you imagine reading the word: *aqua* as in *water, marine* as in *sea*. Finally, a deep blue, the color of pigment, paint squirting fresh from a tin tube. Sylvia Plath, writing in her journal the month she met Ted Hughes, the day, no, the day before: "What word blue could get that dazzling drench of blue moonlight on the flat, luminous field of white snow, with the black trees against the sky, each with its particular configuration of branches?" No matter the snow, the black trees. The sea was that color, the color of *what word blue*.

I was reading Plath's journals that summer because I was twenty-one and daffy with sensation, drunk with it. And for the kind of person who goes straight from a major in English to a graduate program for study of same—that is, for me—*The Jour-*

nals of Sylvia Plath, 1950–1962, republished that year, unabridged, counts as pleasure reading. They met, Sylvia and Ted did, in February, and were married in June, on the sixteenth, Bloomsday. That was on purpose. On purpose and a dead giveaway—that they shouldn't have done it I mean, get married. The youthful symbolism of it. Or one of, anyway. One of the dead giveaways. This was, I was, in Otranto, in August. The sea was three shades of what might have been called blue and I was both on vacation and not.

Camila's parents were Argentinian psychoanalysts and I was on vacation in that they had paid for my flight from New York to London and from London to Rome and from Rome to Brindisi and for the train from Brindisi to Otranto and also for the resort at which we were staying, which was tiered and terraced, smooth-walled and all-inclusive and so theoretically I could order, from the lounge chairs, whitewashed and wooden-slatted, as many drinks as I wanted. Though practically I couldn't because the reason the flights and the train and the room had been paid for, the reason I was with Camila and her parents at all, was that Camila had twin brothers, seven years old, and it was my job to mind them. Matteo and Tomás, Tomás smaller and fairer and Matteo, his torso tanned, his hair dark and curly, always getting mistaken for a local. Because of the name, too—Artemisia's father was Italian, hence the spelling. They lived on the Upper West Side, Artemisia and the boys and her husband, Pablo, they were of Argentinian *extraction*. Camila and I were friends, was another point in the vacation column.

The first two weeks were the hardest. The boys had a nanny back in New York, also Argentinian, but August was her month off, too, and with me at first they had mutinied, as children will do when surrendered to new authority. They couldn't have known precisely why I was reluctant to run from their room to their parents' room, double-checking what it was they were and weren't supposed to be eating and watching, how late they were or weren't supposed to stay up, but they must have sensed it, my reluctance. My all-encompassing apprehension. Artemisia had given me only parameters—not too many sweets; keep an eye on your wine, they'll try to tip it into their Coca-Cola—and a different woman would have understood this as license, a different woman would have known, from Artemisia's eye makeup, from the long shift dresses she wore, sleeveless, from the bracelets that busied her arm, slender and golden, from her sunglasses and scarves, from the fact that Pablo had only ever spoken to me directly three times and never about the children, that the rules were mine to make. But I was an uncertain girl, weak of will and ego, and I wanted Artemisia and Pablo to like me, Artemisia in particular because it was immediately obvious, from her shift dresses and her bracelets and also from the way Pablo angled his head when he spoke to me, so that his eyes, and he was already short, were looking not quite at my face, that her approval would be the harder won. I lived in fear, those first few weeks, that Tomás and Matteo, Teo we called him, so that they were Tom and Teo, the *o* in *Tom* narrow, closed, so that it sounded not at all like an abbreviation for the American *Thomas,* would run to their parents and tell them their new nanny was just awful and couldn't they send her away. Like I was in some knockoff Henry James novel, some knockoff Merchant Ivory adaptation of same.

And so that was the first week, me trying to deny them this treat or that privilege and them complaining and me giving in immediately, buying them *bomboloni* in the morning and *cornetti* in the afternoon and them having no appetite for dinner at eight and demanding to stay up for the eleven-fifteen movie on Retequattro, the boys whining, *So what that it's rated red,* which is how Tom and Teo fell asleep watching *Basic Instinct,* me thinking, Well surely it's been edited for broadcast and certainly it's been dubbed and really how much Italian can they actually understand, even with the fluent grandfather, the cognates. Like the *language* was the problem. I did keep my eye on my wine.

The second week was worse because they'd tired, already, of getting what they wanted, the desire, in these cases, being not merely to get what one wants but to feel as if one is getting *away* with getting what one wants, and so they began to create actual trouble, trouble of the damaging-the-hotel variety, which is how I found myself, on the evening of the tenth night, yelling, for the first time really *shouting* at Teo to stop using the serrated dinner knife to try to liberate the feathers from a pillow. He responded wonderfully, stopped right away and only cried a little, ate his *frutti di mare* quietly, didn't ask after a gelato or a chocolate profiterole. And the whole time: his eyes wide, a small smile on his lips, pink and wet, hoping for a smile in return, a nod of approval. It's true what they say, children really do crave boundaries. By *they* I mean Artemisia.

The day before the serrated-knife incident, early afternoon, the boys, sun-drunk from a morning at the beach, asleep, small Speedos sandy, limbs splayed, breathing deeply, drooling, I'd knocked on Artemisia's door. Come in, she said, and I opened the door and found Artemisia in her bathing suit. Come in, she said again, because I had not yet crossed the door's threshold. I stepped into the room and Artemisia turned away from me, bent to untie the knots of fabric at her neck and at her spine that were holding the top of her bikini in place. Close the door, she said. I did and when I turned back around she was facing me. Her breasts were heavy and low, freckled, her nipples the color of walnuts, roasted, wrinkled, too, in a way that suggested they might have a similar texture. I mean none of this critically. Her nipples pointed not down but ahead. All of this I absorbed in a second, half, my eyes flying up to meet hers. I'm wondering, I said, about discipline. How you usually discipline the boys. The boys, Artemisia said, crave boundaries. All children do. The precise boundaries matter less than the fact of their existence. Tell them, Artemisia continued, what it is they must not do and when they do it anyway, she shrugged, punish them. As she shrugged, her breasts perked and then flattened. Her hands were on her hips and her fingers framed a gentle fullness, not a proper roundedness but a kind of visible exhalation, evidence, the only visible on her body, that she'd twice been pregnant, given birth. Her feet were shoulder width apart and her thighs, also freckled, did not quite touch. Punish them? I asked. I was looking only at her face. Yes, she said, a time-out, no dessert, penalties of that sort. She shrugged again. Though I suspect you will not need to go even that far. If you raise your voice. She smiled. They are timid boys. They are very eager to please. She bent down and I saw she was beginning to remove the bottom of her bikini as well so I nodded quickly and turned and left, closing the door behind me, forgetting to thank her for the advice she had given me, forgetting even to acknowledge it.

So then it was the third week and the boys had gotten used to me and I to them, opposing armies on Christmas morning agreeing to an armistice, trading presents, one *cono alla vaniglia* in exchange for forty-five minutes of playing in the sand, no swimming, Nanny wants to read for a bit. I was watching them from my lounge chair, this was a day or two later, when a shadow fell across my legs. Boundaries, no? The voice belonged to Artemisia. You tell them that they can play in the water but that they must not swim and indeed, that is precisely what they do. I nodded. Teo was splashing Tom and Tom was turning to run. Keep your feet on the sand, I'd said. Stay where I can see you. Artemisia bent and her shadow moved up my body. Sylvia Plath, she said, reading the spine of the book I'd placed facedown on my knees. Not a very good poet, she said. But yes, an interesting person.

It was that night, or maybe the night after, after I'd fed the boys and put them down and had dinner with the family and Camila had left to meet friends she'd made on the beach and Pablo had left to see if he could use the resort's telephone to make an international call, that Artemisia again approached me. I was sitting on the terrace, onto which both my room and the suite's living room opened, a glass of white wine on the table in front of me and also a few sheets of paper. In my right hand a pen, blue, my second and third fingers stained with its ink. Artemisia was wearing a white linen shift and she was carrying a bottle of white and also a glass and she asked if she could sit and when I said yes I could feel the vein in my neck begin to throb, just slightly. I'm not, she said, disturbing you? And when I said no she asked what I was writing and I said, A letter to my boyfriend, and then, Or, not my boyfriend, we broke up, before the summer. This was not quite accurate. I'm going to graduate school, I added. He didn't want to follow you? Artemisia asked. I laughed and she frowned and I said, quickly, It's just that I'm young and he's got a job in New York and it didn't, a helpless hand gesture, come up. If we'd been, and here I paused because I hadn't yet lied outright and didn't want to, didn't want to lie to her, and yet explaining the situation also seemed impossible, but then Artemisia smiled and I stopped talking, relieved. *Ready*, she said. You were going to say, *If we'd been ready*. Ready to get married, yes? This was not what I had been going to say. Of course it was true that I wasn't ready to get married, but this wasn't the problem, the problem was that my boyfriend, who was also my former professor, already was. Nevertheless I nodded. No one is ever really *ready*, she said. She removed, from a pocket in her shift dress, a pack of cigarettes, a brand I'd never seen in the States, Diana, the package white, trimmed in pale blue, and asked, Do you mind? She was already lighting the cigarette, even as I was shaking my head no, no, of course I didn't.

My first husband, she said, exhaling. I met him

at university, in Buenos Aires, while I was completing my bachelor's. I, too, had decided to go to graduate school, for psychology. I had been accepted at Columbia. Very prestigious. Especially for a foreigner. Someone not fluent in the language. She poured herself a glass of wine from the bottle she'd brought, took a sip. I suspect, she said, that Camila's admission was due in part to my own. Given her more limited powers, intellectually. Her lack of extracurricular interests. Though I do not know how heavily a parent's graduate attendance weighs on a child's undergraduate application. And of course Pablo was once a professor there as well. This may have counted more. She took another sip.

It was late, almost midnight. We ate late because of the heat and even now it was still warm enough that neither of us had sweaters on. Artemisia's shift was sleeveless and I was wearing a tank top, spaghetti-strapped, and olive-green shorts with small cargo pockets just above the hem. As she spoke I nudged my tank top down so that no skin was exposed between its bottom and the top of my shorts. My legs had been perched on the seat of the table's third chair, but now, feeling the weight of her gaze on the expanse of my too-pale flesh, I crossed my right leg over my left, hooked my right foot behind my left ankle, tucked my feet beneath my chair. As she spoke I watched her lips move, watched her neck. I wished, despite the heat, for a blanket to drape over my lap so that the contours of my lower body might disappear entirely beneath it.

Artemisia's judgment, what she had said about her daughter, it was harsh but I did not dispute it, both because I believed it to be true and also because I was familiar with the Pérez family policy, which was honesty in all things. If she was telling me this she had certainly told her daughter as well, in the same spirit in which Camila had told me, during our first week in Otranto, that she would rather spend her time with the six young Greek tourists she had met on the beach than with me and her brothers; the same spirit in which she had, during the first months of our acquaintance, informed me that I should never wear heels with straps, even T-straps, because the place on my ankle where the circular strap hit shortened my calf and made it appear not only pudgy but meatlike, not a calf but a shank being served on a platter of shoe. It wasn't that Camila and I weren't friends, it was, precisely, that we were. And if both of us had imagined my taking care of her brothers as a way, the only way, to spend this last summer together, given her money and my relative lack thereof, it was Camila who had first realized that to preserve the friendship she would have to abandon me. Or not to preserve it, for the friendship was lost anyway, in the fall I would go to graduate school and Camila would remain in New York, but to honor its memory. So yes, it's true that when I think of Camila that summer, what I see are the backs of her thighs as she walks away from me, down the beach, toward the Greeks, or maybe they were Germans. But at least I don't see her treating me like the help. This I now consider a kindness. Anyway I didn't dispute Artemisia's judgment, instead I nodded and sipped my wine and Artemisia continued. My boyfriend at the time. I met him at university. He was not a fellow student. He was a professor. My professor. Perhaps now the situation would be seen differently. But at the time I was not at a disadvantage. Or I did not see myself as at a disadvantage. We did not begin our relationship until after I had completed his course. And in any case the problems that developed were not related to this initial power imbalance. She shook her head. Not in my opinion. They would have developed no matter. In any case. But I was saying. When I moved to New York, he followed me. He would not admit to this. He was not the kind of man who would follow a woman to a different town. Much less to a different country. But it so happened that he was offered a fellowship for one year to teach not at Columbia but at Sarah Lawrence. The university gave him a leave of absence. We married. For reasons of a bureaucratic nature. Perhaps visas were easier to obtain. Possibly the taxes were lower. In any case. When I left Buenos Aires, it was with him.

13

We didn't live together, in New York. Sarah Lawrence had already set aside for him an apartment and I refused to commute. And this separation, it—it brought something out of him. A kind of jealousy. The difference between jealousy and envy, do you know it? She did not wait to see if I would shake or nod my head. Envy is wanting to acquire the thing you do not have. Jealousy is wanting to keep the thing you do. It was a side of him I had not seen before. He had been, during our relationship up to that point, Artemisia paused. I was going to say *kind*. And that, too, is true. But the more accurate term is *fatherly*. I did not see it immediately. Did not see that I was looking for a father figure. You see I had an excellent relationship with my father. I still do. And it is usually those who have bad relationships with the parent of the opposite sex who seek a romantic partner to fill that role. Usually, but not always. Because it can also happen this way; it can also happen that one becomes stuck. This is what happened to me. It was my father who had loved me most tenderly, who had shown me the most affection, and so it was he, when I began to separate from my parents, that I sought to replace. And Virgilio was that replacement. Virgilio. Artemisia smiled. Even the name signifies.

In Buenos Aires, we hosted dinners together. He would invite his friends. Professors, writers, poets, ex-politicians, important people. This was 1975, '76.

The beginning of, Artemisia paused, took a sip of her wine. You are familiar with Argentina's Dirty War? I nodded, though in fact the phrase meant very little to me. Paramilitary groups, a coup, the term *desaparecidos*. I could feel the underside of my right thigh growing slick against the top of my left. This was the time, Artemisia said, of the Dirty War. It lent, to these gatherings, a frisson. Well, it lent for me. Perhaps others felt as more—real, the possibility of danger. But for me—a knock at the door, yes I startled, but what I felt, in here, she moved her hand to her breast, it was not fear, she shook her head, it was the feeling the actress has when she is, she lifted her hand and waved it, at the side of the stage, waiting for the line so that she can—for the cue. The sense that we might all, at any minute, be, she moved her hand through the air as if grabbing something. For me it was thrilling. Perhaps you think I am callous, describing things in this manner. Or cynical, frivolous. She shrugged. I am only telling the truth. And anyway, at the time, I was more interested in how Virgilio's friends were treating me. These important people. They were all decades older. And yet they treated me well. Whether at his instruction or of their own accord I have no way of knowing. I suspect he must in some way have prepared them for me. None of them were condescending. Well. The men condescended in the way that men always condescend toward women. What I mean is that I was treated as an equal. Or as much of an equal as a woman could be in that place, at that time. Even when we made love, and here Artemisia stubbed her cigarette out in the ashtray. The vein in my neck was throbbing now and I could feel the sweat pooling under my arms, could feel it dampening the cloth of my tank top, and I nodded because I felt she was waiting for some kind of signal, though in retrospect I think it more likely that she had paused, in fact, for dramatic effect. Anyway I nodded and took a sip of wine. My mouth was dry and the wine tasted bitter. Artemisia lit another cigarette. Even when we made love, she continued, he did not force himself on me. He was in some ways instructive. But always, there was the asking and the giving of permission. But then, and here Artemisia shook her head, blowing from her mouth, as she did, a cloud of smoke, when we got to New York he became— She paused, smiled. There is a Plath poem. You know the line *Every woman adores a Fascist*? "Daddy," I said. That's from "Daddy," of course—I'm reading— Yes, Artemisia said, I noticed, and I blushed because I remembered then that she had. Not a very good poet, she continued, but an interesting person. And the author of a few very good poems, of which "Daddy" is one. Virgilio had been, as I said, a father to me. And now he became a fascist. He wasn't, to be clear, an actual fascist. Though Argentina had plenty in the years after the war. Even my grandparents, my father's parents, well. I was still young when I realized there was a reason they had emigrated from Italy and it wasn't because they had fought with the *partigiani*. But Virgilio, no, he was not a fascist. Not politically and not emotionally or physically, either. Not until New York.

Almost from the moment we landed, Artemisia exhaled smoke, there were signs. Virgilio was not as comfortable in English as I was, and so, when we landed, I was the one who called the woman who had rented me an apartment, I was the one who gave the cab driver directions. I was the one who spoke to Virgilio's department head. My landlady lived in the apartment below the one she had rented to me. She had offered to let me use her phone for the first few days. Just until I was able to get my own line set up. Virgilio went downstairs to call his department head. A moment later, I heard him call my name. The necessary English words were escaping him. He needed my help. Well, it had been a long flight. Naturally he was exhausted. So I came downstairs and he gave me the phone. Artemisia exhaled smoke. Me helping him. I could tell right away that he was finding the experience unpleasant. Whereas he had found the inverse very pleasant. The experience of being the helper, of helping me. At some point the landlady asked if we were father and daughter. Artemisia smiled. Possibly this, too, disconcerted him. And then I began to notice little comments about Columbia. What a shame that it wasn't at the level of Harvard, of Princeton, of Yale. Throwaway comments, but persistent. How it was too bad I hadn't gotten into one of the *first-tier* Ivies. I don't know if he thought he was being subtle. Perhaps he did, if only because I said nothing. I wished to save him the embarrassment. But so perhaps thinking himself subtle, he began to go further. He began to speak about the undergraduates he was teaching at Sarah Lawrence. How exceptional they were. He told me that of course they'd all gotten into Yale and Harvard and Princeton. But they'd chosen to go to a smaller school. A *liberal arts college*. At a liberal arts college, he said, they knew they would receive the full attention of their instructors. And those instructors would of course be full professors. Not underqualified graduate students whose time was divided between research and teaching and classes of their own. He said this all very casually. Or he must have thought he was being very casual. Certainly he could not have thought his jealousy was as obvious to me as it was. His sense of inadequacy. Because still I remained silent. As I said, I did not wish to embarrass him. He had been, Artemisia exhaled smoke once more, ground her cigarette into the base of the glass ashtray. As I said, he had been a kind of father to me. To see him diminished in this way. She paused a moment, shrugged, and I thought of her breasts moving under her shift, perking and then flattening, she was not, I could tell, wearing a bra, for now a light breeze was blowing and I could see her nipples, hard beneath the loose linen. It was difficult, Artemisia said. I felt implicated. I felt myself diminished. One searches, in one's choice of partner, for a kind of reflection. Sometimes consciously, sometimes unconsciously. Often unconsciously. And often not an honest reflection. One searches for a better-than reflection. An as-I-wish-I-were reflection. This is, Artemisia took a sip of wine, knit her eyebrows together, *pitiable* is perhaps the word. *Meschino,* my father would say. Small. But it is also human. Virgilio had reflected well on me. He had shown me to be intelligent, worldly, mature. He had shown me to be older than my years, which is often what young people, what young women in particular, wish for. Perhaps you, Artemisia said, you, too, have wished for this. And now I thought of my former professor. I thought of how the games we had played, me taking dictation from him while—how they had emphasized not my maturity but my inferiority. But in New York, Artemisia continued, he shrunk. And as he shrunk, so did I. At first I remained silent. I was saying nothing. I was ashamed. But then, Artemisia shrugged, something changed. I became a little colder. A little less deferential. A little bolder. I began to treat him a bit like a child. Knowing what someone else does not: this defines the relationship between the adult and the child. The adult knows something that the child does not. And knowing how foolishly he was behaving I began to protect him. From the world, but also from himself. His accent was difficult to understand, so at restaurants, I ordered for him. I helped him set up a bank account. We went shopping together and I picked out his clothes. What I mean to say is that in public it was clear, Artemisia smiled, who it was who wore the pants. She shook her head. So, okay, at first I behaved this way only with Virgilio. With him I was aloof and assertive, and with others humble, shy. But then, again, something changed. It became natural to act in this way at all times, with all people. And I found that, acting in this way, I attracted many men. Many American men. It's a cliché. That the woman who seems not interested, who plays what is called *hard to get*, that she is attractive to men. Any women's magazine will tell you this. Any romantic comedy. But clichés become clichés because they are rooted in truth. At least this has been my experience. Of course not every man will find himself interested in a woman he suspects does not respect him. But many will. Many of the men I encountered did. I did not tell Virgilio about the men who had made their interest clear. Mostly they were other graduate students. But there were professors as well. A few bold undergraduates. But his jealousy. She shook her head again. Jealousy does not need confirmation to flourish.

What followed, Artemisia sighed, from the psychological perspective, it was a natural progression.

She topped off her glass, refilled mine. He began to question me about my whereabouts. To demand that I tell him with whom I spent my evenings and what we discussed and for how long. Now, with cellular telephones, it is easier to demand this kind of accounting. Then, the imposition was more obvious. At that time, I did not even have an answering machine. Just a rotary telephone. And this telephone was always ringing. Often it was ringing when I opened the door to my apartment. And if I did not pick it up it would begin ringing again, ten minutes later. Or five, or three. Sometimes only thirty seconds would pass between the last ring of one call and the first ring of the next. Not always Virgilio. But almost always. During the day, too. When he knew I would be in class. Or at the library. I think he was hoping to catch me in a lie. I tried taking the receiver off the hook, but a couple hours of silence and I would begin to worry that someone else might be trying to contact me, a professor or perhaps even my parents, and I would replace the receiver, and often, not always but often, I would forget then to remove it before leaving for campus in the morning. The phone rang so often that my landlady asked me to speak to Virgilio. And when that didn't work she spoke to him herself. And when that didn't work— Artemisia shrugged. She told me that she would not break my lease but that she could not allow me to renew it for the following year. She said she was sorry but the ringing was giving her headaches. She dreamed only of telephones. Still, Virgilio would not stop calling. Only on weekends, when Virgilio and I were together, was the phone silent.

Finally, Artemisia sighed, one afternoon, I found him waiting for me outside my door. This was a weekday. The building was two stories. The front door opened onto a small landing and on the left side of that landing a hallway led to the door of the landlady's apartment. On the right side were the stairs. Artemisia's hands were moving as she spoke, sketching. He must have knocked on the front door and my landlady must have heard and let him in because that afternoon I found him sitting on the second floor. His head was bowed and his back was against the door to my apartment. I remember my cheeks were flushed. It was late March but still cold. I think my landlady let Virgilio in out of pity. She would not have wanted him to wait outside. Certainly that was why I let him in. By then it was clear to me that our relationship could not continue. I had not yet decided whether that meant it had to end or if its—its terms, the terms under which we were operating, if they might still be transformed. We had not had sex in months. Not since our first weeks in New York. By choice. By my choice. It wasn't that he was controlling—that he was trying to be controlling. In the end this is not what bothered me. It was that his desire to control, she paused. This desire, it stemmed not from his power but from its lack. It was his desperation I despised.

I slipped a cigarette out of Artemisia's pack and she handed me her lighter, poured more wine into both of our glasses. I let him in, she said. She paused. She took another cigarette from her pack, tapped one end on the table, rotated the cigarette, tapped it again. It happened quickly, she said. I opened the door and set down my bag and as soon as I straightened my back his hands were on my shoulders. He turned my body so that I was facing him and then he pushed me against the wall. One hand was on my shoulder and one hand was on my neck. He pushed the door closed with one foot. This all happened in a moment. I felt his hands on me, I gasped, and by the time I'd finished inhaling, by the time I was beginning to exhale, Artemisia shrugged. The door was closed. She lit her cigarette. Normally, this is where one would say, *You can imagine the rest*, no? But what I suspect you would not be able to imagine is this: I felt scared only for that moment. The moment of the gasp. Then the door was closed and I was exhaling and what I felt was relief. Relief and also excitement. Because the power dynamic that I was familiar with had been reestablished. As I said, in Buenos Aires, he had been a kind of father figure. But then in New York, I had played the role of the adult. I had protected Virgilio as a mother protects her child. I was the one with hidden knowledge. With under-

standing. With *power*. But the introduction of violence, Artemisia exhaled. The effect was regressive. I
was again the child.

He left immediately after. I think he was ashamed
of what he had done. Virgilio was by nature a gentle man. I imagine that his actions confused him.
I waited until I could be sure that he was back in
Bronxville. And then I called him. I said it would be
best if we did not see one another again. He did not
argue. He said very little during our conversation. As
far as I know, he left New York at the end of that
semester and returned to Buenos Aires. The two of
us never spoke again. Artemisia smiled. Actually, we
never divorced. I met Pablo soon after. He was a professor. One of my friends was in one of his classes.
We fell in love and got married and I became pregnant with Camila. All of this happened very quickly.
When we applied for the marriage license, I said I
had never been married.

Artemisia paused. The relationship I entered
into with Pablo, she said, the marriage we have. It
is very like the early stages of my relationship with
Virgilio. Only I was secure from the beginning in
the knowledge that it would not change. Pablo had
lived in the States longer than I had. His reputation
here was already made, was growing. I could build
a career of my own without fear of overshadowing
him. You know, we are both now well established,
and still, Pablo is better established than I. I do not

mean to imply, Artemisia said, that my marriage is perfect. Pablo has had his girls. And I have had mine, my girls and my boys and my men. We do not deny each other these, she moved her hand, passing pleasures. Only that it works, my cheeks were flushing, for me. For me it works perfectly. But this is not what I wanted to say. For a moment she held my gaze, exhaled smoke. What I wanted to say, she said. The so-called *rape fantasy*. Most psychologists, Artemisia said, theorize the commonality of the so-called *rape fantasy* among heterosexual women as linked to shame. Heterosexual women and also non-heterosexual women, when indulging in heterosexual fantasies. Women are raised to believe that they should not desire sex. More explicitly in earlier generations, yes, but the message remains, implicit, today. The difference between *slut*, for example, and *player*. The word *player*, in her accent. Not that she mispronounced it, the mere fact of the word, in her mouth, also because she was an adult. The sound instantly and unavoidably wrong. Briefly I felt, as I had not before, embarrassed for her. The connotations of each word, she said, and how each is applied, across genders. All this you must know. Artemisia waved her hand, trailing smoke. But okay, the rape fantasy. At least theoretically, it allows the woman to have the sex that she desires without also having to admit to the shame of that desire. Force becomes a method of circumvention. A shortcut. But, and here she leaned in, this was not the case with me and Virgilio. It was not because I was released from shame that I found relief in his violence. It was because I was released from *control*. Artemisia paused and exhaled smoke and took a sip of wine. Of course it was crucial that I did not fear Virgilio. I did not believe he would truly hurt me. And this made it possible to appreciate the, she smiled, *initiative* he took. To take pleasure in it. I have, she exhaled smoke, never wanted control in my interpersonal relationships. I have only wanted to be cared for. This is what I realized, on the afternoon that Virgilio appeared outside my apartment. Romantically, sexually, economically, I have always wanted to give myself over. And I could no longer give myself over to Virgilio. Not because he was violent. No, precisely the opposite. The outbreak of violence was a sign. Artemisia took a drag of her cigarette, exhaled. It was a sign he was losing control. And violence was the only way he could think to reassert it. A temporary solution. In showing me his strength, he was also showing me his weakness. His embarrassment, afterward, this confirmed it. It was not that I was scared of him. It was that I was not scared *enough*. Artemisia looked at me then and our eyes met. She stubbed out her cigarette. The heat pulsing through my body, at that moment, I called it *admiration*. Admiration because Artemisia knew herself so well and I, at twenty-one, did not, had not yet settled on the governing narrative of my life. Had not yet realized the folly of governing narratives. The certainty of Artemisia's voice, this is what I was responding to. It is what, remembering her story, remembering that summer, knowing that folly, I still, unwilling, respond to now.

Respond to but don't trust. What I mean is that Artemisia *seemed* to know herself. *Seemed* because Artemisia was less master of her fate, captain of her soul, than she was a clever gardener. Sequestered in a domestic plot, she worked with the tools at her disposal. Trapped, yes, but in a hedge maze of her own careful design. How else to interpret her insistence that she had never wanted control? That she had, in her relationships with men, only ever wanted to be a child? How else to interpret her insisting all this to someone she barely knew, to someone who was still a child herself? Though sometimes I think in fact she did know herself. Sometimes I think one of the things she was trying to tell me was that she was unhappy in her marriage.

Artemisia was, at the time of our conversation, no older than forty-four. In other words, she was young and yet, because of my age, she seemed to me old, even quote-unquote wise, and therefore untouchable, metaphorically but also literally, and so even as I was coveting her sleeveless shifts, coveting the stern knot into which she'd tied her long hair, streaked with gray, the few frizzed locks that had escaped the grip of her elastic, it did not then occur to me that I might also be coveting the body beneath and below. Now I know that I am never more covetous than when someone tells me a story, a secret, the sharing of a confidence stoking in me the hunger for intimacy of a more proximate kind. I'm trying to say that Artemisia's mouth was moving. That if I had been capable, in that moment, of true honesty, I would have said that what I most wanted to do was stop it with my own. I'm trying also to say that this desire need not be, was not in this case, sexual. Not in the way that the term is commonly understood. Artemisia had, in telling me her story, given me something of herself. My desire to kiss her was a desire to thank her, was a desire to give her something of myself, was a desire to become her, the imagined gesture equal parts grateful, generous, acquisitive.

Artemisia lit one more cigarette and smoked it down. She drank the last of her glass of wine. The bottle she'd brought to the table was empty. Well, she said, I should go to bed. Good night. She stood and then bent, placed one hand on my shoulder as if about to confide something further to me, something of so delicate a nature it would need to be whispered, her mouth moving against the skin of my ear. Perhaps I imagined, in the next moment, her head bowing as if to meet mine, the dip of her torso. Because then she merely pursed her lips and gave my shoulder a squeeze and, gathering her cigarettes, her glass, the empty bottle, reentered the suite's living room and went, I assume, to her bedroom, the bedroom she shared with Pablo. I say *shoulder* but in fact she placed her hand in the curve where shoulder becomes neck. Let it, though perhaps this too I imagined, linger. I did not see her again that night.

Ann Arbor, 2002

There's this girl I know." She took a drag of her cigarette, exhaled. We were in her apartment, large but the space poorly apportioned, two bedrooms, a bathroom, and then a kitchen jutting off a wide central hallway that served also as the living room, its floor hardwood, dark and scuffed; earlier that night I'd ripped a hole in my stockings, snagged the soft fabric on a splinter. I was sitting on the floor. We were graduate students in the Midwest and our stipends had rented us more space than we knew what to do with. John had been at the party but he had left and it was only women now, four of us: me (female pain in Jacobean revenge tragedies); the apartment's tenant (American literature since 1981); Laura (the Bloomsbury group, with a focus on Virginia Woolf); and a blonde with heavy eyelids, those eyelids now closed because she was, her head resting against the wall, asleep (female narratives of the Civil War). Because Laura and the tenant were on chairs and I was on the floor and the other woman on the floor was asleep, I felt myself an acolyte or a novice, felt Laura and the tenant to be my teachers. Mostly the tenant. I craned my neck. The tenant was speaking.

"This girl I know. Knew. We went to undergrad together. We weren't close, but I'd see her around. Not at parties, but in class, or she'd host—she called them *soirées:* cheese and crackers and flaky puff pastries stuffed with meat—and I'd be invited. We had coffee, lunch, a handful of times. Nice girl. Mousy, shy. Had braces her freshman and sophomore years. Pretty. But unpolished. Hair always back in a ponytail. Overalls. Actual overalls. Like the nerdy girl before the makeover, the makeover that is destined to be, that is *a priori* successful, because the girl, of course, she was always hot, she was just"—she waved the hand holding the cigarette—"wearing weird glasses or whatever." She stubbed the cigarette out. "Anyway, her junior year, this was after the braces came off, she started dating this guy. She was—" The tenant stood and walked into the kitchen to refill her drink. Behind me was a coffee table littered with discarded cups, plastic, most of them, a handful filled with cigarette ash, lipstick-smeared butts. The tenant was standing now, leaning against one edge of the arched threshold that divided the kitchen from the hallway–living room. "She was," the tenant said, "a virgin. I don't know how I knew this—I don't think she told me—but I'm sure I knew it and

31

I'm sure it was true. We were part of the same larger circle. All of us English majors." She smiled. "One semester a whole bunch of us took Chaucer and we would spend our weekends getting drunk and memorizing bits of *The Canterbury Tales*. We had a game going where the thing was to sneak the word *queynte* into conversations with anyone who hadn't done their pre–eighteen hundreds pre-reqs." She shrugged. "I guess you'll just have to trust me when I say I'm sure, when I say it was known. Not that we gossiped about it. We were twenty, twenty-one, and I mean we memorized Chaucer for *fun*, it wasn't so unusual. Just, it was known." The tenant lit another cigarette. Laura and I were still sitting. Laura was worrying a cuticle on a finger of her left hand with the thumb of her right, as was her habit when she was no longer and could not foresee when she would again be the center of attention. The blonde made a small noise somewhere between a sneeze and a snore and rolled her head so that it drooped now over her left rather than her right shoulder. "But anyway this guy. He was—we wouldn't have known to call him a predator then. A *sexual predator*. Even now, saying the words, I feel kind of"—she shrugged again—"kind of stupid. But he was a grad student and my first year he dated a freshman and then later she dropped out and my second year he dated another freshman and she went on medical leave and in between there were"—she waved the hand that wasn't holding the cigarette—"rumors. That he could be a little—rough. That he didn't care if the girl wasn't into it. That the pretty girls in his section got the best grades. I remember hearing once that he had a wife stashed away somewhere, but that one I never— Anyway. The point is, my third year, our junior year, this girl, she starts dating this grad student. And the fact that he was dating a junior, this actually seemed like an improvement. She was twenty-one and he was thirty-one, maybe thirty-two, and we, I feel bad about this now, we joked that maybe this was exactly what she needed, like he was the hot guy in the movie about the pretty nerd, how she wouldn't be a virgin much longer. I want to say—I want to offer as *exculpatory evidence,* our fear. I want to say that our jokes were born of our relief that he'd picked her and not one of us, and I do think that was part of it, but also— she was so prissy, she didn't drink, didn't go to parties, turned all her papers in on time. I think we resented her for being—apparently, of course, not like we knew—untouched by college, unmarred. By this point, this was several semesters post-Chaucer, we'd all humiliated ourselves in one way or another, gotten too drunk and vomited in the bushes or yelled at an ex in the backyard of a frat house or woken up in someone's bed and not been able to remember how we got there—but this girl; this girl, she hadn't—not once. We resented her for it. And then also why *hadn't* he picked us, that was the other side of it, weren't we good enough, pretty enough, smart enough. By what criteria had we been judged, in which ways had we been found wanting.

"Anyway. We told ourselves she must have known what she was getting herself into. We told ourselves she was an adult, and sure the rumors were widespread, sure they were widely believed, but they were also just that, rumors. The porn wars were over and porn had won and we were porn-positive, we were sex-positive, we probably wouldn't have even called ourselves feminists. Who were we to judge." The tenant walked over to the chair she'd been sitting in and began to lower herself, changed her mind, stood back up. "At first," she said, "at first they seemed happy. He started going out a little bit less and she started going out a little bit more. Once a month, twice a month, we'd see them at a party together—she'd always be wearing something ridiculous. Once, this was in March or April, nowhere near Halloween, she came in a kind of—classy cowgirl costume, patterned dress, lace trim, hat and boots and a ribbon around her neck." She shook her head. "But so anyway they'd show up, arm in arm, and she'd be wearing something ridiculous and she still wouldn't drink, just sit on the couch and sip from a cup of tonic water all night while he took shots with former students. Now I tell my undergrads, told my undergrads, If a grad student wants to hang out with you, that's a sign, a sign you should definitely *not* hang

out with them, but back then"—she shook her head—
"it didn't occur to us, how inappropriate it was, this
guy at parties with people a decade younger than he
was, people whose grades he had recently been, in
some cases still was, responsible for. We thought it
meant we were—mature, sophisticated, I don't know,
adult." She lit a fresh cigarette off the butt of the
one she had finished, left the butt in a plastic cup
to smolder. "Anyway, we thought it said something
good about us, his being at our parties, rather than
something evil about him. But okay this girl—so at
parties she'd sit on the couch and she wouldn't really
talk to anyone, just sit and sip and watch, but also
she didn't seem unhappy. She had this smile like
she was"—the tenant made air quotes with the hand
that wasn't holding the cigarette—"'happy, with a
secret.' I heard that somewhere. I've always liked it.
'Happy, with a secret.' The safest way to be happy, if
you think about it. If you keep it a secret, the happiness, it's harder for someone else to, you know"—the
tenant shrugged—"take it from you."

She paused and while she paused I had two
thoughts. First, that the phrase "happy, with a
secret" did not necessarily imply happy *because* of
a secret, did not necessarily imply *keeping the source
of happiness secret,* could just as easily indicate happy
and *also, unrelatedly,* keeping a secret and, second,
that I was pretty sure I knew where this story was
going, not only because the man in the story had

been identified as a *sexual predator* but also because it was late and it was only women and we were all a little drunk and under those conditions there is only one place a story about a boy and a girl ever goes. So I knew where this story was going and I was thinking that I wanted her to get on with it, get it over with, but also, as I looked up at the tenant, who was standing, sipping bourbon from a mug, taking a drag of her cigarette—there was now a layer of smoke in the hallway–living room, a halo hovering four or so feet off the ground, the tenant at its empty center—as I stared up at the smooth slope of the tenant's throat, at the declivity above her collarbone, a further thought entered my mind, not a thought but a wish, specifically the wish that she *not* get on with it, get it over with, stop talking. The wish was that she would go on talking so that I could go on staring. She was two years ahead of us, us being me and John and Laura and the blonde, wasn't teaching anymore, on dissertation fellowship, and I liked to imagine her days, their discipline, her waking up and making coffee and sitting down in front of the computer with a stack of books, liked to imagine the glass of wine at six o'clock, the cigarette on the porch, a book in hand, reading for pleasure now, chopping cloves of garlic, an onion, sautéing them in a cast iron pan; she would know how to season a cast iron pan. I didn't know her that well, this tenant, this not-girl, this woman, but she was slightly older and very beautiful and she carried herself like she was one body, a whole, not a collection of disjointed limbs, and for this reason I believed her to be very intelligent and I was in awe of her and a little bit in love with her and also I loathed her, not furiously or passionately but attentively, careful to keep the flame of—it wasn't quite hatred; something closer to envy, something tinged with lust—anyway, whatever flame I was nurturing I was nurturing it with care, so that, on this night as on all nights, it was burning fierce.

But she was speaking again. "This went on," the tenant said, "for months. Six months, maybe." She counted on her fingers. "November, December, January, February, March, April. So yes, six. And then it was May. And all this time the girl had remained a virgin. I don't know how I knew this but I did know it." The blonde hiccupped in her sleep. The seat Laura had been occupying was now empty. "Middle of May, there was a concert. Middle of campus, four bands, day drinking. We mixed mimosas for breakfast, stashed martinis in water bottles, laid out blankets on the lawn. All day I drank orange juice, ate olives. Someone had a baguette, sliced meats. They were on a blanket near ours, this girl and the grad student. She was wearing what looked like a maternity dress, a length of green cloth, short-sleeved and high-necked, brocade detailing across the chest. Her hair was down and her cheeks were stiff and pink

37

from smiling and the freckles on her neck, down her forearms, dotting her ankles, they were shining, they were giving off some kind of heat, she was glowing. It took me a second to realize she was drinking a beer. The grad student tucked her head under his chin and turned to me and winked." The tenant paused. She stubbed her cigarette out, swallowed the last of her bourbon, sat down. She'd been, as she spoke, standing, pacing, moving from the chair to the arched threshold and back. The bathroom door opened and Laura appeared, wiping her hands on her jeans. The blonde was snoring. "You know how this ends," she said. "That night there was a party. Big house, two floors, five bedrooms. Or, they were using five bedrooms. Five were upstairs but there was one downstairs, a spare. It was ten or eleven by then and she was bright and loud and dancing, arms everywhere, and then she was unsteady on her feet, and then she was sitting on the floor and the grad student came over and put his hands under her arms and lifted her up and carried her to the spare bedroom. He said he was going to put her to bed, let her get some sleep, it was too far to carry her home, or maybe he didn't say anything, maybe that's just what we all allowed ourselves to believe. I was drinking bourbon. Some Beatles song was playing and we were all singing along. I was doing the twist. I only ever did the twist in college, never any other kind of dance—letting other people see my body in ungoverned motion, it seemed too chancy. You know—" She paused for a moment and when she spoke again she was speaking more quickly: "I didn't drink before college, had greasy bangs, wore long skirts because I hated my calves, wouldn't wear pants because I hated my thighs. We should have been friends. If not friends, allies. Instead I hated her. Her vulnerabilities, her weaknesses—she wasn't hiding them and because she wasn't hiding them I felt she was exposing me, too. Maybe the grad student sensed this also, our kinship, because when he left the spare bedroom, fifteen, twenty minutes later, fiddling with his belt, he caught my eye, raised an eyebrow. He didn't say anything, just went back to the party. When people started trickling out, he went back to the bedroom, woke her up, gave her a glass of water, walked her home. But we all knew. Maybe the next day a friend of mine talked to a friend of hers, or maybe someone saw her crying. Somehow it was confirmed, though I didn't need confirmation, I understood the moment he raised that eyebrow, the moment he left that bedroom, the moment he entered it." The tenant cleared her throat, stood, began collecting cups and mugs from the coffee table behind me, taking them to the sink. "I only thought of her because she was in the paper today. The *Times* had her wedding announcement." I gathered a few cups and brought them into the kitchen. "She's a writer," the tenant said, "freelance.

39

She published a book review in *The New Yorker*, I read it, recognized her name. And she was smiling in the picture. The engagement picture. She was. Only the smile"—the tenant's back was to me, she was washing a mug out, but I could see her shoulders rise and fall—"of course it was a portrait, posed, but still the smile was different. That's all. That's all I really wanted to say."

I walked home alone. Laura and I shared an apartment but I insisted on staying to help clean up and anyway Laura wanted to walk with the blonde, was worried about her getting back to the floor-through loft she insisted on calling, with faux modesty and technical accuracy, a "studio." I wasn't a smoker, that is to say I smoked only other people's cigarettes, and before I left, I bummed three from the tenant, lit the first inside the apartment and chain-smoked the second and then the third on the short walk to my building and then in my building's courtyard. As I walked I thought of a thread being cut, of two fingers snapping. What was it a hypnotist said when it was time to awaken his patient? An image in black and white—a man, portly and mustachioed; a woman, supine; a pocket watch swaying—and the phrase *You are getting very sleepy.* He made her stand and squawk like a chicken and the audience laughed and then she woke up, and she didn't understand why her fists were in her armpits, why her right leg was raised. Maybe he just clapped his hands? Strange that I couldn't remember because of course that was the awful part, not the bit where you squawked but the bit when you realized you were squawking.

There were things that horrified me about the story—the raising of the eyebrow, for example, and how afterward everyone knew. Knowing that afterward everyone knew. And the act itself, of course—wrong, that was indisputable, criminal even, and further degraded by the choice of location. But also, walking the length and width of the courtyard, trying to keep warm, wishing I'd taken the tenant up on her offer of what remained of her pack—"Really you'd be doing *me* a favor, every cigarette you smoke is a cigarette I don't smoke"—but also wasn't there, beneath the details, something—to be overwhelmed, to have no choice in the matter, wasn't there something— Obviously not if you were drunk. Obviously not your first time. Obviously not if you didn't, somewhere deeper, somewhere—less acceptable and so less accessible, really *want* it. But no, that was what they said, what rapists said, that the girl, the woman, had really *wanted it.* So no, in addition, there would—I mean there would have to be some kind of *understanding,* it couldn't be just the man's— But if there was. I mean, mightn't it, couldn't it— To be in someone else's power, not to have to make decisions, to be in fact prevented from making *all* decisions except where to move your—in fact maybe those

decisions *also* were being made *for* you so that— I
had finished the third cigarette. Something to do
with being chosen, something to do with release of
responsibility. Could what the graduate student did
be wrong and what I sometimes felt I wanted also
be right. I crushed the butt beneath my heel. Was
it nostalgia I was feeling or was it guilt. Either the
desires I had were possible desires and these desires
had been fulfilled—either I had allowed these desires
to be fulfilled, either I had encouraged, had chased
their fulfilment—or, this was the other option, I had
been tricked. The other option was I was wrong. The
other option was I could not trust myself, not how
my stomach fell and then how my muscles tightened
around the place where my stomach had been, not
how the blood drained from my face and how cold
sweat pooled under my armpits. Either there was a
way to see this so that—or else there was something
fundamentally— But really it was so cold. And the
twenty-four-hour convenience store was too far to
walk to and anyway I wasn't a smoker. There were
maybe two fingers of bourbon left in the bottle
on my dresser. It was so late. I would go upstairs. I
would drink the two fingers and maybe one of the
beers in the fridge. I would remember to brush my
teeth. I would put on my pajamas and get into my
bed. I would go right to sleep.

San Francisco, 2010

The museum was hosting a Swedish video artist's first American exhibition. This Swedish
video artist: her work is largely about female
pain. By *female pain* I mean *female subjugation* and
exploitation, and *humiliation.* By *female pain* I mean *her
pain.* She makes, in her art, a spectacle of herself.

I drove down the coast to the museum and at the
museum, I met my friend. My friend, tall and dark-
haired. She kept her sunglasses on when we went
inside. She had broken up with her boyfriend and
called me and I had driven down. She had been crying all morning. "Fiancé, I guess. I never wore the
ring." Rather: he had broken up with her.

Did I, do I, admire the artist for claiming her pain
is worthy of art, or did I, do I, find the act of aestheti-
cizing also trivializing, or in fact is that feeling, that
impulse to call the art *trivializing,* a way to conceal
the true feeling, guiltier, that her art is *vulgar,* that it
is *indulgent,* because she is her own subject? Because
she elevates herself *as* subject? The woman as object

is less vulgar than the woman as subject. The woman as object is art and the man who objectifies her an artist. The woman as subject, well. Just a narcissistic bitch, isn't she? Not that I believe this. Not that I do not believe this.

In one room of the museum a series of screens had been mounted. On one screen: a ballerina in pink and her male partner in black, his hands firm about her waist. In the eighteenth century, the ideal wife's waist was no larger than the span of her husband's hand. On another: two opera singers, one male, one female, mouths open, chests heaving. Bad luck if your husband had short fingers, diminutive palms. On yet another: a stage, a curtain, red velvet, drawn, and a woman, pacing, declaiming on the proscenium. At her heels, nipping and barking, a terrier, brown and white. Occasionally the terrier reared up on its hind legs and pawed at the tails of the woman's button-front shirt. There were more screens—a man and a woman running hurdles on a track; what might have been a job interview, with a man, suited, behind a desk, if not for the woman before him, her hair shorn, her body encased in sackcloth—and, next to each, a pair of headphones.

Several years before, the Swedish video artist had divorced her husband. Her second husband, I am moved to say, in the spirit of pettiness. I am, myself, once married. The day I met my friend at the museum, I was not yet divorced. The Swedish video artist and her husband had two children together. During the divorce proceedings, the husband sued for full physical and legal custody of both children. He charged that his soon-to-be ex-wife was an unfit mother. The case went to court. Several videos by the Swedish video artist were entered into evidence. There she was, in a bathtub, naked, bleeding from between her legs: a miscarriage. In her hands, a copy of *The Odyssey*. She reads from Book Twenty-Two, the slaughter of the suitors. There she was, in chain mail, in the kitchen, preparing dinner. *Beneath the chain mail*—this is her husband's lawyer—*I will draw your attention to the fact that beneath the chain mail respondent is completely nude.* She serves dinner—bowls of soapy water; a salad of unwashed weeds; uncooked spaghetti, halved, covered in motor oil—to a family of blow-up sex dolls. She goes into another room and retrieves a sword. With the sword she decapitates each sex doll. Then she sits down at the table and begins eating the dirt-covered weeds. In court, during the Swedish video artist's testimony, the judge seemed unable or unwilling to look her in the face. Her husband, I should say, was American, as was his lawyer, as was the judge, and it was of course in America that this trial took place. In Connecticut. The Swedish video artist was granted supervised visitation: three hours, twice a week. She chose, in defiance of the custody agreement, to return to Sweden.

45

To *abandon her children*. I am quoting contemporary press accounts, though it is always possible that I am quoting them inaccurately. The day I met my friend at the museum I, myself, did not yet have a child.

After the trial was over, the Swedish video artist obtained a transcript of her exchange with her ex-husband's lawyer. She made copies of the exchange and distributed these to a handful of female artists she respected: a choreographer, a librettist, a playwright. There were others: a filmmaker, possibly also a poet, possibly also a rhythmic gymnast. She asked them to choose performers they themselves respected. And then she filmed the performances.

At the museum, at the far end of the room in which the screens had been mounted, above one closed door, wall text, the letters large, black, press-on, the font a sans serif: "The Story of the Children." I tried the knob of the door and found it would not turn. Presumably this was a metaphor.

"It seems," my friend said, "like cheating. They do all the work, and she gets the show."

"It was her idea."

"If she were a man, you'd call this exploitative."

"But she's not. Historical context. It matters."

"The point of feminism," my friend said, "isn't to replicate existing power structures, only with women in control. Or it shouldn't be."

"How did you get here?"

"I called a car. You know public transportation here is—"

"And presumably you know that saying the words *existing power structures* doesn't mean you're not part of the problem?"

"How was I supposed to get here, then?"

I twirled one finger in imitation of a game-show wheel. "And the winner is . . . biking! One of very few ethical modes of transportation—provided of course that the bike was, when you purchased it, used. You should have biked." Do my words sound cold, even cruel? Perhaps it helps to know that as I said this, I was smiling.

"And get my clothes all sweaty? No thank you."

"Your choice."

"How did *you* get here?"

"My car's electric."

"Your car's a hybrid. Excuse me, your *husband's* car is a hybrid."

"Same difference." I would not call us, my friend and I, liars. Nor would I call us, in general, honest.

"Patently false." Instead I would say that one of the premises of our friendship, a friendship that I have, in the years since our visit to the museum, let lapse, was that we were honest if with no one else then at least with each other. And that to force this honesty, we were compelled also to be cold, also to be cruel, to each other.

"Are you saying," I asked, "that you'd rather I wasn't here?" Also that this cruelty was, for us, a way to commune. A source, even, of joy.

"No," my friend said. "Are *you* saying you'd rather *I* wasn't here?"

Isn't that the test of love? The test of intimacy? The willingness to be cruel and the belief that, the moment of cruelty passed, the love, the intimacy, remains, undamaged?

"No." Yes, it is.

"Good."

Or at least I have at times believed this to be the case.

"Good. Now. Do you want to tell me about your breakup."

My words were phrased as, but in fact were not, a question. My friend rolled her eyes. Rather: she made the head motion—from left to right and then up a tick, her skull sketching the shape of an upper-case *L*—that I associated with her eye rolls, which were frequent. I could not see her eyes because she was still wearing sunglasses. "Well. What do you *think* happened."

"He found out you were cheating on him."

"Correct."

Another of the premises of our friendship was that we loathed emotional intimacy even as we understood its necessity. Speaking with casual nonchalance about subjects that caused us great pain was our preferred workaround.

"If you were a man, I'd call you a cad."

"Sure, if this were the nineteen fifties."

"I'd be ethically obligated to take the wronged woman's side."

"If I were a gay man? Or a lesbian, for that matter. Or a straight man, but trans. Say I were nonbinary, or my partner was."

"I'm just saying. The point of feminism isn't to replicate existing power structures only with women in control."

"You don't say."

"The fact that you're a woman cheating on a man doesn't make the cheating itself any less morally reprehensible."

"Precisely what Paul told me this morning."

"Really?"

"No. He said, Now I know why you never wanted to wear the ring."

In another room, a number of enormous photographs, perhaps six feet across, twelve high, were displayed. A series of portraits of the Swedish video artist. There she was, wearing a mustache, a uniform, individual hairs glued to the swatch of flesh between the first and second knuckles of each finger. There she was, stooped, in a polo shirt, pale blue, on her head a gray cap, gripping a cane, tan slacks cinched tight above a prosthetic paunch, tendrils of white hair emerging from beneath her cap. And there she was, in a flannel shirt and jeans, bringing an axe down on a log, her hair short and dark and stiff with Brylcreem. Not Brylcreem. Brylcreem is British. Its Swedish equivalent. Next to each portrait, a smaller picture, also framed: snapshots of a man in the poses the Swedish video artist was replicating. Her father, the wall text revealed.

"Daddy issues," my friend said.

"You or her?"

"That's the name of this exhibit."

"Funny."

"Barely."

Facing the photographs, along the opposite wall, a full, functional bar: bottles, tender, the whole nine. My friend and I approached.

"Eleven-thirty," I said, checking my watch.

"A mimosa?"

"Two mimosas," I said.

"I'm sorry, ma'am." This was the bartender. "At the artist's request, we have stocked a full bar but are only serving one drink: George Dickel, on the rocks. That's a whiskey, ma'am. A particular favorite of the artist's father."

"I *know* Dickel's a whiskey. And don't call me ma'am." To my friend: "Too early?"

"Never."

"Two, please."

We sipped our whiskeys. "Tell me," I said, "how he found out." Important to imagine us, here, backs to, elbows on, the bar. Not looking at each other.

"I used his computer to check my e-mail." Staring, instead, at the photographs across the room.

"And you forgot to log out." Staring straight ahead.

"Forgot. Sure, that works."

"You wanted him to find out."

"I did."

"Why?"

"You want to know a funny thing?"

"Always."

"I wasn't even cheating on him."

"You mean technically? Like, you hadn't had sex?"

"No, I mean it was all—" My friend made a shooing motion with her free hand. "The guy I told you about, the one I was cheating on Paul with. I made him up. I made it all up."

"The e-mails that—"

"I wrote them. From a different address, of course. It was fun, actually. Thinking up a character, his job, the words he would use. Where would he suggest we get together. Did he prefer *pussy* or *cunt*."

"And when you told me. That you were having an affair."

"A lie. He preferred *pussy*, by the way. That's when I knew it wouldn't work out. Vile word."

A slight increase in the effort involved in keeping my face still. My friend's revelation had apparently pained me.

"*Cunt* is the better word, that's true." The revelation of the lie, I mean. Because beneath the first premise of our friendship was the understanding that we were, both of us, bad people. Or that we believed ourselves to be bad people. What's that old line? Ah, yes, now I remember: Every adult in the Anthropocene who is not too stupid or too full of himself to notice what is going on knows he's a real piece of shit. We believed that, and the fact that many others did not, this was, wouldn't you know it, a real barrier to intimacy. In a deliberately even tone: "Is it worth asking why."

My friend shrugged. "I don't know. Is it?"

"Okay. Why?" And if my friend had been hiding this from me, she might also have been hiding other things. And if she had been hiding this and also other things from me, it was perhaps because she thought I was not bad *enough,* felt I could not understand her most evil deeds. And if she thought that, well, our honesty had served no purpose, for in that case it was clear that she did not understand me at all.

"Bored, mostly."

"Have you considered getting a job?" My friend had, has, family money.

"I have a job." This was an argument we'd had before.

"You don't." The fact of my friend's family money meant that I loathed her, just a little, for political reasons. Also that I let her pay for dinner.

"I volunteer."

"Why not tell him?"

My friend shrugged again. "Boring. What time is it?"

I checked my watch. "Noon."

"Another?"

"Why not." To the bartender: "Two more, please."

In a separate building, my friend and I entered a small gallery temporarily pressed into service as a changing room. We took off our clothes and put on bathing suits. Back in the building's main gallery, we entered the swimming pool that had been installed at its center. It was a Monday, midafternoon, and the pool was otherwise empty. The bottom of the deep end was not tile or plastic or ceramic or stone. Instead it was a video screen. On the video screen the Swedish artist appeared naked, also in a pool. The perspective was such that her pool seemed to be located directly beneath ours. Such that it seemed almost possible to move from our pool into hers. I reached out with one hand. I touched screen. The Swedish video artist's mouth was moving. She was saying something, I think, though it was impossible to hear her, to know even in what language she was speaking. Then my lungs were burning and I came to the surface. My friend rose, too. Her eyes, if they had been puffy before, now weren't. The irises blinked green. I had, until that moment, forgotten the color of my friend's eyes.

We exited the pool and dried off.

"What did you think?" I asked my friend.

"Nice tits," she said.

"I mean the concept."

"Did you notice the name?"

"*I Have an Important Message.*"

"Obvious, don't you think?"

"Yes," I agreed. "A little obvious."

Los Angeles, 2011

My parents live in Los Angeles, in a shambling three-story in the Hollywood Hills. Inherited, my mother's father's mother a minor star, silent films, with what they used to call a Cupid's-bow mouth and a smart bob, she bought the house with her first paycheck, financially savvy and good thing, too, didn't survive the transition to talkies, or maybe it was giving birth to my grandfather, how the pregnancy changed her body, the softness around the middle she never lost. Don't like it, them, my parents. Talking about them, I mean. Not being modest when I say shambling, my grandfather and my mother, both only children and too good for any kind of regular work, the house decaying and no money for repairs. There's a picture on the wall along one of the staircases, not a picture, a page from an old tabloid, framed, newsprint, a shot of my great-grandmother, in low heels and a dress with no waist, on the arm of Rudolph Valentino. I have been, in my life, just close enough to wealth to touch the rotting lace of its hem. Another way to put this: my family has been, still is, richer than most.

What happened was my friend got divorced, and then, for a while, she went to live with my parents. She said, my friend, that she wanted to spend some time with people who liked her. I lived in California too, though up north. With my husband, though my friend did not ask if she could stay with us. I guess I was a little offended. Told myself she wanted to be tended to, knew I would not tend to her and knew my mother would. Though also I was relieved. Just then we were trying to have a baby. Baby books everywhere and me lying on my back, in bed, a thermometer in my vagina, trying to take my basal body temperature so I'd know when to fuck my husband, this, we'd been told, was the most natural way. My mind so filled with this one desire—baby, baby, baby—it might as well have been blank. Dutiful copulation. Tension and resentment packed into each of our small rooms like pudding into pudding cups. "Do you think," my friend asked me, "that it's ethical, right now, to have a baby. Considering where we are. In late capitalism, the life cycle of the planet." I hung up. My husband and I did not end up having a baby, though not for ethical reasons. Later we also got a divorce. Having a baby, in any case, is never ethical. I don't mean it's not, just that's the wrong scale.

"How is she," I asked my mother.

"Oh, a little brittle," my mother said. I could hear

the clink of ice, a gin and tonic I guessed, almost seven, a weeknight, would be her second. "And sad of course, but that's normal, that's only natural. You know we were talking, yesterday—the day before yesterday?—and I was telling her—" is where I stopped listening. My friend, you'll remember her, Laura, thinks my parents like each other and this may also be true, but mostly they are just drunk enough not to be bothered.

I met Laura in graduate school, where I also met my husband. They were dating when I met them, Laura and my husband. My ex-husband. That's not true. I did meet both Laura and my ex-husband in graduate school, but they weren't dating. That would be a better story. I am often thinking of the better story because the actual story is so often boring. We were in the same cohort, and we became friends, the three of us. I was dating a professor at the time. Sleeping with. That sounds like a good story but it's not, it's been told too many times. He had a beard and a jacket with those elbow patches. I wish I were joking. Made good martinis, had hollow cheeks, explains the beard, hated his ex-wife. All pretty standard.

After grad school, my husband and I ended up in the same city. That makes it sound accidental. Actually I couldn't get a job and the city where my husband, future then ex now, was moving because he could and did was also a city where I had some family. The city was Lincoln, Nebraska, I don't know why I'm being so cagey. I mentioned this to my future then ex now and he said, "Come," he said, "we'll split a two-bedroom," he said, "Do you even know how cheap rent is in Lincoln," and I said, "Actually yes I do my uncle lives there." We'd all gone to grad school straight out of undergrad so even five years later we were still pretty young. The reason I couldn't get a job was I hadn't finished my dissertation. Still haven't. Anyway so I moved. That was when we started dating, me and the future then ex now. Not that it matters. Laura got a fellowship in Michigan and we moved to Lincoln and we fell in love. Who falls in love in Lincoln.

Laura met her husband in Mississippi. After grad school she got a fellowship in Michigan and after the fellowship in Michigan there were two years in Arkansas and then a spot opened up in Mississippi, Oxford, Ole Miss. Not an academic, the husband, but he ran a bookstore, managed it, was well read, which we cared about then, whether someone had read the same books we had, and which I try to, have to, care less about now. Hadn't gone to college though, which made Laura's choice unusual. Exotic, even. How she told me, breathless, on the phone, that he'd worked in construction, and not just during the summer for extra money between semesters but as a job, full-time, for years. They met and were married in nine months. And then some time passed and Laura's contract was up and she got a new job, tenure track, in California, and her husband, his name was Dylan, he didn't want to leave. Laura moved in with my parents right after she filed the paperwork.

What I care about—what I try to care about—now. A sense of humor. Kindness, whatever that is. Knowing who the good teachers are, knowing how to get my kid into their classes. I did have a kid, eventually. A baby who is now a kid. Not with my ex. Not with anyone. I mean, not with anyone who's still around.

So Laura got divorced and moved in with my parents and after a while I went down to visit. We went for a hike in Griffith Park. The winter and the first half of that spring it had rained, really rained, for the first time in years. Thunderstorms taking drivers on the 405 by surprise. Record snowpack in the Sierras. This was June and people were skiing. In Griffith Park the bloom had peaked in March but wildflowers were still sprouting, an embarrassment of petals, yellow and burnt sienna and ripe purple, pale green stalks. The top layer of earth was a soft powder, a light brown so anonymous and uniform as to appear, in memory, colorless, and Laura talked and I listened. I walked ahead of Laura because I am by nature a competitive person and also because Laura was talking and so slightly out of breath. She talked about Dylan. I'd only met him once, at the wedding, their courtship had been so rushed and then also their marriage.

Dylan had been raised by his aunt and uncle. His mother had died in childbirth or just after—an infection contracted at the hospital, not as rare as you'd think—and his father, devastated, had driven from Belzoni, Mississippi, to Salina, Kansas, the baby in a drawer liberated from the bedroom dresser, and knocked on his dead wife's sister's door. At least, Laura said, this was how she imagined it. The father driving the eleven hours straight, though of course he must have stopped for gas, to feed the baby. The drawer part was true, Dylan had told her that, said the aunt and uncle still had it, though this didn't make sense to Laura, wouldn't Dylan's father have needed the drawer, back home. But Dylan had shrugged, said probably he'd been too ashamed to ask for it back. Didn't spend the night, had a cup of coffee then he was back on the road. Dylan swore his father hadn't called ahead, hadn't asked his sister-in-law and her husband whether they wanted to take the baby, take him. Laura had asked and Dylan had shaken his head, back and forth, his head drooping so that Laura could see the bald spot, a perfect circle, like a timid monk's tonsure, blooming at the tip of his skull. I loved that bald spot, Laura said, that soft underbelly he carried at the top of his head.

We were drinking whiskey, Laura said, and it was late. All I did in Mississippi, Laura said, was drink whiskey. Summer nights, we'd drive out into the country, start with beer, Budweiser, nothing fancy, then a beer and a shot, the beer going down easy, like water, the condensation on the bottle being the real point, how cool it was against my hands, my neck, you know out in the country even the bars didn't have air-conditioning, just ceiling fans, if your skin was dry you could barely feel the breeze. The whole state was like a proof of concept for the idea of sweating. By the time he got to this part of the story we were drinking whiskey straight. We'd known each other a few weeks then and he wasn't trying to seduce me, he didn't need to, for one, we fucked the night we met—the word *fucked* here standing in for Laura's anger, I stumbled as she said it, small rocks on the path coming loose under my feet as it came snapping out of her mouth—but also it wasn't the story you'd tell if you were trying to get a woman to sleep with you. It was the story you'd tell after, when you'd decided you wanted to sleep with her again, and again after that, maybe wanted to keep sleeping with her for a while, but also you were a man and so you couldn't come right out and say it because telling people what you want makes you weak. That, Laura interrupted herself, I actually believe. Telling people what you want, *speaking desire,* and I could hear the air quotes in her voice, the ones she used when she slipped into grad-school vernacular. It's like telling people how to hurt you, handing them instructions.

I think, Laura said, the fact that women are better at asking for what they want, that we have to be otherwise we'll never get it, and even then, even asking, mostly we don't, I think this is why we're stronger than men, in general. But anyway, Laura said, what Dylan said was after his mother died there was a funeral, and at the funeral his aunt asked if they, if we, needed any help and my father said we would be fine. My father, Dylan said, was a man of few words. Probably he was still in shock and didn't know it, that's what my aunt said. So six months went by and every week or so my aunt would call my father to check in on us and every week my father would say we were doing just fine, thanks for asking. And then one week my aunt called and my father didn't pick up, the phone just rang and rang and the next day he was at my aunt's house, we both were, him in a suit looking sheepish and me in the drawer, overheated. They thought I had a temperature but I was just swaddled too tightly. My aunt thinks he had a breakdown. I think he came to his senses. I think, Laura said, that's the night I fell in love with him. If he'd asked me to marry him that night I would have said yes. It wasn't the story itself but how he told it. No anger in him, just sorrow. Sorrow not for himself but for his father, how scared he must have been. His father was dead by the time Dylan moved back to Mississippi. It wasn't forgiveness in his voice. Laura shook her head. It was more, it was beyond, it was like—like forgiveness was something he could turn around and look at, like that's how far in the past it was, like that's how still it was for him, how sure. And I thought that was beautiful. It was a religious feeling I had, sitting across from him, like I was in the presence of something holy. And I don't think I was wrong, but I do think I saw him for a moment and thought I'd seen him whole, only that's not how it works, is it. The whole is the whole, the moment can't stand in for it.

By this time we'd hiked to the top of something—a ridge or hill, not a proper mountain—and so we paused and stood together for a moment, silent, looking out. Also, Laura said, I didn't realize how many times he'd told the story. I should have known, how polished it was. The practiced hesitations. I thought he was opening a door. And that on the other side of the door was—intimacy, I guess. Only it was just a room. A crowded one. Laura made a sound like she'd started to laugh but forgotten how partway through. I looked at her. Since we'd reached the top of the hill or ridge I had only been half-listening, had been thinking, instead, about what it would feel like to push Laura over the edge. I mean literally. Not that I was angry at her. Just, I'd been having these kinds of thoughts. On the freeway, looking at the bumper of the car in front of me, at the low fence separating asphalt from dirt and then rocks and then ocean. Thinking the word *temptation*.

On balconies and sidewalks, my mind flipping back and forth between *jump* and *push*.

It might be worth mentioning that at that moment I hated Laura, was glad her marriage had fallen apart, that her ceaseless trust in the world had at last been proven foolish. Finding friends in every city she moved to, marrying a man on the strength of what, who knows, everywhere manufacturing happiness, happiness, happiness. But her luck had run out. Her story was still the better story, but finally, thank god, she was miserable in it.

Also that I'd started involuntarily imagining what it would be like to fuck every man I came into contact with. What it would be like if the power went out and everyone else in the room were raptured and we just had to do it right there on the conference room table for the sake of, you know, humanity, his hand in my hair, pulling, and me opening my mouth to protest, the words dying in my throat. Involuntarily, right. I was working in HR at this point, is that irony. I should know, that PhD I didn't finish was in English lit. Probably this was connected to the fact that I'd started watching porn. Every morning, right after taking my basal body temperature, like putting a thermometer in my vagina gave me the idea. Like I couldn't think about making a baby without thinking about making a baby. In retrospect I think I was mad at my husband. Is that too obvious? Remarkable how hard it is for women to admit they're angry. Not annoyed or upset or irked or miffed or any sentiment that might be captured in a text message that ends in a series of exasperated question marks. Angry.

The fantasies I kept having, I hated not the form of them but the content. Not that they were pornographic but that they were clichéd, that even the sex I let myself imagine was boring. Another cliché: my husband was having an affair. No, not another cliché, a lie. Actually I cheated, and not on a conference room table post-rapture, in a hotel room, there's the cliché, up in the city, San Francisco. Then I came home and told my husband. This was later.

Up on the ridge or hill I turned to Laura and said, "Why did you tell me that story?"

"I think," she said, "I thought I was telling you a story about how we fell in love."

We started back down the path. "What do you think the story is about now?" I was again in front of her and so had to turn around to ask this question.

"Sometimes I think it's a story about being tricked. Not that he did it on purpose, but it wasn't accidental, him confiding in me, just then." Of course every confidence is a kind of manipulation. Or calculation. *I trust you with this.* Or maybe it's *I want you to* think *that I trust you with this.*

"And other times?"

"A low bar. I'm not—I mean, your mother dies and your father abandons you, I'm not saying that's not rough. But the man tells me one sad, you know he shares one feeling—not even, he sort of *implies* emotional depth, and I'm ready to marry him. We ask too little. Or I do, anyway."

We got to my car and I drove Laura back to my parents' house. She asked me if I wanted to come in and I said I didn't, But tell them I said hello. Then I drove back up north, to Marin County, which was where we lived. You know Marin County, clogs and herbs in window boxes and cleaning with white-wine vinegar. Inconveniencing ourselves, yes, but only if we were guaranteed an aesthetic payoff. Good intentions, sure, but when have they ever been enough. And my herbs were dying. Some wanted water and some wanted sun and some wanted shade and a good talking-to and I couldn't bring myself to care which ones were which. Anyway even the aesthetics we could barely afford, how we thought we were going to manage with a child I have no idea. When we split I moved in with my parents, my husband had to get a roommate.

Two things Laura said: the part about *speaking desire* and also the part about the low bar. I started thinking about how I'd told John, that was the future then ex now, I wanted a baby, and he'd said *Okay,* like that, no conversation just *Okay,* like it was my decision, how endlessly supportive he was every month when I got my period, never angry, never sad, like it was something that was happening not to us but to me. And then I thought about how what I wanted was not a baby, not a baby with John, what I wanted was to go into the glass-fronted cabinet we'd bought at an antiques fair and restored, John was handy, he had that going for him, all those summers working construction, and remove the tea service his parents had gotten for him, for us, a wedding present, Limoges china, floral pattern, delicate handles, those rims so thin you wanted to bite right through them, and smash it, smash every single piece. Twelve cups and twelve matching saucers and the teapot, bulbous, mocking me. A bizarre gift, his parents weren't particularly rich or particularly British, something they said they thought I'd like. Maybe because I was, am, a snob.

So I opened the cabinet and I took the teapot out but then instead of smashing it I set it down on the ground and I removed its dainty lid and I unzipped my jeans and I pulled down my underwear and I pissed in it. Wiped the spray away with the bottom of my T-shirt, put the lid back on. Lifted the teapot, put it back in the cabinet, closed the cabinet's glass-fronted door. In my hand the china felt, just slightly, warmer.

The piss stayed in the teapot for a year, my last year with John. Then I had my affair and I got my divorce and I gave John the teapot and now I live somewhere else with my kid. He's a boy. I haven't seen Laura in years.

San Francisco, 2012

"Twice a month." A smirk. "Maybe three times. Three days, two nights. Usually Tuesday to Thursday, though sometimes I'll pull a Monday–Wednesday, a Wednesday–Friday." I was on the bed, he was on a gray armchair. "Wednesday–Friday, that's the shit. Thursday's the weekend but with plausible deniability. It's weekend pussy but no missed soccer games, no wife on my case about date night, no *you don't spend time with me*, no *you don't love me anymore*. None of that crap." He'd loosened his tie and unlaced his shoes and he was drinking scotch from the minibar.

"Can you hear yourself?" The armchair was all curves, not a right angle on her. Upholstered in velvet, which had to mean velvet had swung all the way back around, gone from classy to chintzy to classy again. Earlier I'd asked him a question.

"Hear myself what?"

"*Weekend pussy. Wife on my case.*" The heels of his shoes grinding into the carpet. The carpet plush and white. Would show a stain and hold it, that carpet would. The question had been, *How often do you travel for business?*

"So, what the fuck? What's wrong with the way I talk?"

"What's wrong with the way I talk?" I rolled my eyes. *"What* deleted scene in *which* Scorsese are *you* from."

"This is why the CEO won't let broads on our floor." He set the scotch down, stood. "Guys need to be able to let off some steam, use language."

"Use language," I said, two fingers doing air quotes. *"Broads."*

"The fuck's wrong with the word *broads?"* He paused. "Wait, time out." He crossed his arms. "Do you actually hate this?"

"You're asking? This isn't part of the—"

"I *said* time out."

"No."

"No you don't actually hate this?"

"No I don't actually hate this."

"So why are you—"

"You're being a dick. I'm responding to you being a dick. That doesn't mean I don't like it." My dress was in the bathroom and I was wearing the hotel's bathrobe and under the hotel's bathrobe I wasn't wearing anything.

"That doesn't mean you don't like it."

"No, it doesn't—but okay, *now* you've fucked it up." A pause. "Throw me a bourbon, will you?"

He walked to the minibar.

"That was what, investment banker?"

"Hedge fund." His back was to me now. "That *is* how they talk, you know." Either his voice was muffled because he was facing away or, annoying possibility, I'd actually *wounded* him. I resisted the urge to roll my eyes.

"I don't—I wasn't—" I shook my head. "Forget it. I trust you, forget it. What's next."

"You choose." He tossed me a mini-bottle of Bulleit and I caught it, unscrewed it.

"I hate making choices." My voice just a little higher. The *a* in *hate* held half a second too long.

"What if"—he looked at me—"I gave you direction." Coming out of his sulk then, good boy.

"I take direction"—my eyes on his, my body shifting against the bathrobe against the duvet cover against the duvet against the sheets—"very well."

"Noted." Stepping closer to me. "Filed."

"So. Give me direction."

"Let's say"—a step closer, his hands on the duvet, his torso over the bed now—"as far from stockbroker as you can get." His face level with my face, his hands moving up the duvet. "Let's say none of that generic bro bullshit. But let's say you still hate him. Have good reason to hate him."

"You think I want to fuck someone I hate."

"Let's say I do." His face very close to mine and

then turning. He stood up, retrieved his glass of scotch, raised it. "Let's work from that assumption."

"Okay," I said, "give me a minute." A pause, a slug from the mini-bottle. "Okay," I said, "let's say he's a vegetarian. Let's say he's a feminist. A *Marxist,* even, but like, totally *willing* to consider the ways in which class just *might* be affected by gender and race. Calls his mother twice a week and says he was *raised by a strong woman,* says it one-hundred-percent unironically. On the first date, tells you his favorite novel is *The Golden Notebook.*"

"Is what?"

"Is *The Bell Jar?*"

"Not even a male feminist is that dumb."

I rolled my eyes. "You know it's actually—but okay, fine. Not *The Bell Jar.* And not *The Awakening,* either, and probably not *House of Mirth* because he skimmed a thing about how Edith Wharton maybe hated women and that gave him, like, a bullshit ex post facto excuse for not having read her. Okay, so that leaves us with—oh, *wait,* oh I've got it"—almost spilling bourbon in my excitement, catching myself in time—"so he makes a *point* of telling you his favorite poet is Adrienne Rich but he's really only read, like, a handful of her essays in some anthology or whatever because of course he thinks poetry is like, *so* bourgeois, but Rich is such a great feminist he figures—"

"Wait, so is Adrienne—"

"No, wait, no"—my hands flying up—"it's actually perfect that you don't—but shut up now, you'll ruin it."

This was before Tinder. I had booked a room at a midlevel chain near Fisherman's Wharf, an Inn of some kind, a Holiday or perhaps a Comfort, or maybe it wasn't an Inn, maybe it was a Hilton. Honestly I don't know, I made and canceled the reservations so many times, and always at a different chain. Then I told John that I was visiting a friend from college. That I had a job interview, two days, the company was putting me up. Girls I went to high school with were in town; a riot grrrl group was on a reunion tour; there was a speaker series whose speaker I was just dying to see. All of these things I told him only then my quote-unquote plans kept quote-unquote falling through when I lost my nerve, so many plans and so many times that I can't remember, now, which one quote-unquote didn't.

John was on a health kick, had been, and to spite him I'd been buying frozen pepperoni pizzas, Confetti Cupcake Pop-Tarts, going out for groceries and coming home with buckets of KFC. These were, to be clear, for me. They were to spite *him*, but they were *for* me. He'd open a can of soup, Amy's Organic, while I picked a chicken wing clean with my teeth. As the soup heated, split pea maybe, barley vegetable,

John would chop a head of kale. The night before I drove down to the city, the soup was black bean chili. The soup was heating and John was chopping his kale and I was mauling my wing and every so often I paused, a finger fishing for gristle between my teeth. "It's not," I said, "like it's going to help."

"Help what?" he said.

"It's not like it's going to help your sperm count." Chewing, fishing, chewing. "Their motility."

"I know." Dumping the kale in, stirring. John didn't have a low sperm count. Nor were his swimmers slow, in fact they were fleet of fin, but I refused to go to a doctor to get checked out so it was up to him to devise alternate solutions to the problem of our infertility. "But it's not like," John continued, "it's not like eating healthy is going to hurt." Then: "You want some kale?"

"No," I said. "No, I do not."

I didn't want a baby. But that must be obvious, what I mean is I had never wanted one. I moved to Lincoln and I got married and my husband got another job and we moved and my husband got a third job, tenure track, and we moved again. I worked in HR. I came home from my job in HR and I cooked dinner for my husband. I cooked dinner for my husband and for his professor friend and for his professor friend's wife. If I was lucky, the wife wasn't also in HR. And I wasn't going to finish my dissertation, this was clear. I wasn't going to finish my dissertation and publish it, I wasn't going to be a professor, I wasn't going to get tenure and go on sabbatical, I wasn't going to spend three months in Barcelona perfecting my Spanish, doing archival research. (I spoke no Spanish, what research could I be doing in Barcelona, my area was seventeenth-century English plays.) I wasn't ever even going to live alone. And that's what I thought about when I thought about what I'd lost by abandoning grad school, by marrying young, by following John from job to job to job: I thought about living alone. I thought about sitting on a porch, on *my* porch, as evening fell, sitting there with a glass of wine and a book and empty hours ahead of me. So okay my life was going to be suburban, it was going to be upper-middle-class, it was going to be so far up normal's ass that it came out the other end holding a white picket fence and an American flag. (John's job was all wrong for this, Marin was all wrong for this, no matter, I was angry, I was on a roll.) So okay it was going to be not only normal but *normative*. And the normative thing to do, now that we were settled, now that John had accumulated professor friends who came with pregnant professors' wives, now that every single one of my female coworkers had two at home and was trying for a third, the normative thing to do was have a kid. And I thought that maybe if I chose it, if I told myself I wanted it, if I made the baby an object not quite of desire but certainly of obsession, I might be able to trick myself into liking a life whose comfort I knew even then was so relatively excessive as to be almost criminal. So I told John I wanted a baby and we started trying and even now the part that most surprises me is how long it worked. Probably it was because we had so much trouble; nothing is more desirable than that which is being withheld.

But then of course it stopped working. It stopped working because I didn't want a baby, and now I was mad at John, too, mad at myself for saying *I want a baby* and mad at him for believing me or humoring me or both. Knowing someone, it's one part divination, two parts force. Figuring out what the other desires, that's relatively easy. Giving the other what she desires, getting her to take it, that's harder, or it is when the other is me. Though with John I would have settled for divination. If he had said, *You don't want a baby.* If he had said, *You don't have to be a mother.* If he had said, *You shouldn't be a mother,* maybe—but no, John was ever so understanding. John was waiting for me to figure out what it was that I wanted and he was waiting for me to tell him. He was waiting for the moment when he could say that what I wanted was just what he wanted, too. And so there we were. Every month he said, *You know we can talk about stopping, if you want to stop,* and I said, *I know.* Every month he said, *I don't want this if you don't want this,* and I said, *I know.* Every month we fucked three times a day for two days, the two days I was ovulating and therefore most fertile. Those were the only times I let him touch me.

So I booked a room at a midlevel chain and I drove down to the city. The room was standard issue. Thin carpet in a dull dun color that already looked dirty. That *always already* looked dirty. You can take the girl out of the grad school but you can't take the grad school out of the— Anyway the carpet looked dirty and that was on purpose, that was so you couldn't tell if it was. Also polyester bedspread in a floral pattern, hypoallergenic pillows with the tags to prove it, bars of soap no bigger than fun-size chocolates, thimblefuls of body wash and shampoo and conditioner. I dumped the clothes out of my suitcase and changed into a black dress, tighter on me now than it had been when I'd bought it, vulgar on top. I'd been lucky, the Pop-Tart weight had settled in my tits.

The plan was to walk south, toward Union Square, to walk until I found a hotel and a bar stool and someone on the bar stool next to me with a room key and none of the obvious markers for sociopathy. There's always someone, or so I'd been led to believe: on business or in the doghouse or out on the proverbial prowl. That was the danger of being a woman, or one of them, vulnerability to advances, a danger I'd felt clever about turning, this once, to my advantage. Like I'd invented the art of getting hit on. The hotel bar, the hotel room, this was to avoid the more obvious dangers, those associated with getting into a car, going up to an apartment, following a man to a second location.

I took the Bulleit I'd packed and poured a splash into one of the small plastic cups the hotel had thoughtfully provided, drank it straight sitting on the edge of my bed, my dress pulled up, my ass bare against the polyester bedspread. The dress was too tight to sit down in comfortably. I was counting on not having to sit very long, was, for that reason, not wearing underwear, priding myself, as I drank, for my presumable foresight, for my efficiency.

What would I call myself. I pondered this as I walked south. My shoes were painful enough that I should have taken a cab but I was trying not to waste any more money than was absolutely necessary. Ashley or Crystal or Madison. Darla or Felicity or Joy. Last name Jones or Smith or Johnson. A name that announced itself as fake, just in case the ring and the no underwear and the eagerness to get up to his room didn't give me away. Or maybe I could just, I was smiling now, maybe I could just, laughing now, cracking myself up, just lean in real close and whisper, one hand on his knee, whisper, *No names*.

I don't remember the hotel I decided on, honestly I don't, but this next part I do, this next part is true. I remember walking the square, putting one foot in front of the other. My shoes were tight and the skin they exposed was swelling, red and plump, the soles of my feet slick with sweat. Neon lights, a revolving door, a tinkle of jazz, innocuous. Nodding to the doorman, marble floors, following gilded arrows to the bar. Granite countertops, booths upholstered, leather bar stools. This is what I remember. It was nine, maybe ten. I heaved myself up, plunked myself down. I'd had two fingers of bourbon back at my hotel, maybe three. Three and a half.

I was teetering on my stool, trying to put as little weight as possible on my ass, my shoes scrabbling for purchase on the footrest, when a bartender came over, eyes narrowed, asking, Can I help you, ma'am, asking, Would you like a glass of water? I was sweating, chunks of damp hair spilling from the messy bun I'd wrapped, sticking to my forehead, obscuring my eyes. I sat and exhaled and felt the back seam stretch but not break. I loosed my bun and shook my hair out, leaned over the bar, friendly, saw the tension in his shoulders ease, saw his eyes, alert, flick from my face, mascara smudged, lipstick flaking, to my tits. "Water, yes, thanks," a hand in my hair, rearranging. "I must look *such* a mess, gave the cab driver the wrong address and had to walk *blocks* and it's so *misty* outside." I get southern when I mean to disarm. When he came back with the water he was smiling and his shoulders were all the way down and his eyes lingered on my tits like this time he wanted me to notice. "Thank you *so* much." Smiling at him when his eyes flicked back up to mine, letting him know I knew, that I was flattered, that he wasn't in any trouble. "And a gin martini, please, Hendrick's, dry, dirty, two olives. Three if you can spare them," and by now I was sure he could. Being careful not to lean too heavily on the accent, to speak clearly without overenunciating, to keep one hand in my hair, fluffing it, lifting it off my neck. At the far end of the bar, a man in a dark suit signed his check, pushed back his pint glass, stood. I looked at him and he looked away. It *had* been foggy outside, some of the moisture in my hair *was* water, mist, it wasn't all sweat, the walk hadn't been *that* long. Inside my heels my feet were cooling but where the edges of the shoe leather cut into my flesh I could feel not blood but that clear, slick, sticky substance that precedes it. My martini came and I drank it, ordered another. A different man in a dark suit approached the bar, saw me, swerved away, or maybe this was my imagination, maybe he'd always, maybe he'd *always already* been headed to the bank of elevators. The bartender came over to talk and I did shy, I did bashful, until he went away, I wasn't interested in the bartender. Fifteen minutes passed. Maybe twenty.

I don't remember him sitting down. The door opened onto a hallway that opened onto a lobby, if I'd been turning to look every time I heard footsteps I wouldn't have been able to drink my martinis so quickly. Besides which I didn't want to seem too desperate. I mean more desperate than I already

appeared, a woman sitting alone at a bar, not looking at a book, not thumbing at her phone. It was the
situation we'd all, the girls of my generation, been
warned against, been warned, specifically, against
getting ourselves into. In my adolescence, this was
the early nineties, the women who marched with
Take Back the Night were still hysterical, consent
wasn't yet affirmative, and though *no means no* was
the standard it was also understood that it wouldn't
protect you. And so we were told to keep to well-
lighted streets. To carry pepper spray, a whistle. To
keep keys between the second and third, the third
and fourth, the fourth and fifth fingers of our domi-
nant hands. No short skirts and watch your drink
and tell a friend where you're going and call her when
you get there and again when you get home. When
we thought about sex we thought mostly about ways
to defend against what we didn't want instead of
ways to pursue what we did. So that now the way I
thought to attract a man was to make myself vulnerable to attack: sitting alone, drinking too quickly, my
legs bare and my shoes no good for running and the
hem of my dress riding up. I'd made myself a sitting
duck and deliberately because men were attracted
not to predators but to prey, not to strength but to
weakness, this is what I was thinking when I felt a
hand on my upper arm, the grip gentle but the splay
wide, the fingers thick, promising. "Is someone," he
asked, "sitting here," another hand gesturing to the

bar stool next to mine. I smiled and shook my head, bowed it to indicate, Please, yes, go ahead. Thinking, Better not to speak just yet, better first to figure out what it is you want me to say.

He sat, unbuttoned his suit jacket. "Can I get you something to drink?" he asked. I tipped the dregs of my second martini into my mouth, smiled. "Sure," I said. "That would be lovely," I said. "Thank you." Still trying to speak clearly without sounding like I was trying to speak clearly. He was handsome in a midlevel-chain-hotel sort of way, standard issue. Square jaw, slope of cheekbone, hair. Or that was my first impression but then he turned to me—he was waiting for his drink and he turned away from the bar and toward me and then I could see that his face had been tilted ever so slightly along the vertical axis so that his right eyebrow, his right nostril, the right half of his mouth, the entire right side of his face was a millimeter, a millimeter and a half, higher than the left. The effect was not unattractive.

It's because of this asymmetry that I remember his face. And it's because of this asymmetry that I then took the time to look more closely at his clothes, at the blue suit he was wearing, which was single-button and slim-cut, the legs tapered. And noticing the suit I noticed the tie, pale yellow, flowers embroidered in a baby blue thread, and the glasses case he rested on the bar, next to the rocks glass into which the bartender had poured a generous portion of Johnnie Walker

Blue, and the burgundy socks, visible for an inch or so below the hem of his blue slacks before they disappeared into his shoes, which were dark brown and polished and obviously real leather. And if the shoes and the fact of his suit and the Johnnie Walker and even the hotel bar itself, if all these details pointed in one direction, the direction of *finance*, say, of *mid-cap mutual funds*, of generic *business*, the others, the tie and the socks and the cut of his suit and especially the glasses, pointed in another, in the direction of *sense of humor*, of *reads novels*, of *was never in a frat*. Also reassuring was the ring, thick and gold and on the correct finger. "So," he said. "What brings you to San Francisco?" "Oh," I said. "You know. Work. A work thing." I tilted my head closer to his, blinked slowly. "You?" "Same," he said. "Same."

In his room I started laughing. He paid for his drink and the martini I hadn't finished and the two martinis I had and he took me by the arm and he guided me to the elevator, guided me inside. The elevator ascended. He unlocked the door to his room and went in and I went in behind him and turned to close the door and when I turned back around his body was against mine, his hips against my hips, and he was bringing a hand to my face, his thumb moving down my cheekbone, and I opened my mouth and then I was laughing. I didn't mean to laugh. What I meant to do was move my lips very close to his ear and say, *Let me slip into something more comfortable.* An appropriate line, ever so apropos. But I couldn't get— I started laughing and— Not giggling, really *laughing.* He stepped back, frowning, the frown emphasizing the asymmetry of his face. And then I couldn't stop. Thirty seconds, forty-five, sixty, ninety. A hand against the wall, bent over, chest almost to knees, gasping for air, water leaking from my eyes. Meanwhile he was standing at the foot of the bed, watching me.

"Are you," he said, "are you okay?"

"Oh," I said, "oh, god, I'm sorry, of course I am, of course I'm fine, it's just"—now I was hiccupping, shaking my head—"I'm so sorry, it's just—" He was still frowning but in the frown I now read not surprise but worry. I cleared my throat. "Can you," I asked, "can you get me some water?" He went into the bathroom and I heard the tap running. When he came back he was holding a glass of water, an actual glass. I took it from him, drank. "Do you think," I said, my head down and my eyes tilted up, this was bashful again, though now it was only partly feigned, "do you think you could order me some room service?"

He moved toward me. "You want me to order you room service." I was still in the foyer, the hallway of whatever floor it was, the closed door at my back, a closet to my left.

"Yes," I said, "room service. Isn't that the deal? Buy a girl a meal first?"

"Oh, sweetheart." He smiled, shook his head. "You've got the line wrong. It's 'Buy a girl a *drink*,' and I bought you *several*."

I set the empty glass down on the floor. The water was working, I'd stopped hiccupping and when I rolled my eyes the room didn't spin. "But I'm *hungry*." I reached for his belt buckle, the implication, I hoped, obvious but not explicitly transactional.

He paused. I imagined the calculation: what time it was now and how long room service would take and how long, on the other hand, he would have to wait, downstairs at the bar, for another dumb, damp duck. Possibly also the calculation was monetary: what would I want to order from room service versus what and how much the next girl would want, would need, to drink. And then a decision, him saying the word "So," again lifting his hand to my face, again moving his thumb down my cheekbone, apparently this was a *thing* he did, now his thumb was moving to the edge of my mouth, to my bottom lip, "So. You're *hungry*, are you."

I nodded. I didn't roll my eyes. I opened my mouth, just slightly.

"Well in that case"—I bit down on his thumb— "let's get you something to eat."

It sounded like a come-on but he did order me a cheeseburger and fries, let me take a shower while we waited. I scrubbed my armpits, my feet. I thought about leaving not because I was afraid but because I was ashamed, the little-girl voice I'd used, the words *but I'm hungry,* even now, impossible not to cringe, remembering. But I didn't. No, I turned the water off, put one of the bathrobes on, swiped under my eyes with two squares of toilet paper, my lipstick was a lost cause but the liner smudged across my lids looked plausibly smoky, left my dress hanging on a hook meant for towels.

When I came out of the bathroom the food had arrived and he was in the gray armchair, a glass in hand, an empty mini-bottle of scotch from the mini-bar next to him. I settled myself on the bed, one hand holding the room-service tray, one hand managing the edges of the bathrobe. I squirted ketchup on the burger. For a while we were silent. What I mean is we didn't talk, and also I tried to chew with my mouth closed.

Then he said, "I want to know why you're here."

"Same reason you're here," I said.

"You don't know why I'm here."

"Then why don't you tell me."

"Take that bathrobe off and I'll show you."

I coughed into my burger. "Excuse me, too direct."

"You're in my hotel room, wearing my bathrobe, and you're saying *I'm* being too direct."

"Look, I'm still *eating* here."

"Fair"—one hand going up in surrender—"fair."

I put the burger down. "I'm going to use some

toothpaste I saw in the bathroom," I said. "You think about your answer."

When I came out of the bathroom, he was standing in front of me, one hand braced against the interior of the door's frame. Try not to think the word *menacing*. I took the glass of scotch from his other hand, nudged him back toward the gray armchair, nudged him and he went. In the bathroom the bathrobe had shifted, had slipped slightly so that it gaped away from my body when I leaned forward, facts I was not unaware of as he sat back down, as I stood over him.

"Why," I said, sipping his scotch, "are you here."

"I'm here," he said. He closed his eyes. "I'm here because"—he smiled—"because every so often I need." His hands clenching and unclenching, "Every so often it becomes important," his hands under the bathrobe, moving up my thighs, "to be someone else," his hands at my hips, pulling, "someone other than myself," his eyes opening, the smile becoming a grin.

I stepped back and after a moment his grip loosened, his hands fell away. I handed him his glass of scotch. "Who do you want to be?" I asked.

"Doesn't matter," he said. "Just, not myself."

"Just not yourself." I was sitting on the bed now, the burger, half-eaten, and fries, barely touched, on a tray next to me. "What if I helped you?"

"Helped me how?"

"Figure out who to be."

"Put the tray on the ground." I put the tray on the ground. "You want to help me figure out who to be." I nodded. "You'd like that." I nodded. "Say you'd like that."

"I'd like that."

"Okay," he said. "I'll be someone," he said. "And you tell me"—I nodded—"how much you like it."

"Don't ruin it." I lowered my hands.

"I won't," he said. "I know," he said. A pause, then: "Can I take off my tie?"

"Why are you asking?"

"Because," he said, his eyes wide, his eyebrows furrowed in a pantomime of sincerity, "because I want to make sure. I want to make sure you're comfortable with this. I want to make sure you're comfortable with everything I do."

"Oh I hate this already."

"So," he said. He was blinking slowly. "Can I?"

"Oh I *hate* this."

"Can I take off my tie?"

"Oh this is *perfect*." He was already fussing with the knot.

"My tie," he said.

"Yes," I said, "yes I am *comfortable* with you *taking off* your *tie*."

"What about my shoes?"

"Yes."

"Yes, what?"

"Yes, you can take off your shoes."

His burgundy socks were bright against the white carpet. "I'm taking off my shirt," he said.

"That wasn't a question."

"Can I take off my shirt."

"That was *phrased* as a question but actually I didn't *hear* it as a question? The way the voice is supposed to lift? At the end? Of an interrogative? I didn't actually *hear* that?"

"Can I," he said, "are you *comfortable* with me *taking off* my *shirt*?"

I said, "Yes," but his shirt was already off. His undershirt was white cotton, crew-necked. "If you leave it there on the floor," I said, "it's going to wrinkle." He was standing at the foot of the bed.

"Can I take off my belt," he said.

"Yes."

"Can I take off my pants," he said.

"Yes."

"Can I kneel on the bed," he said.

"Yes." My hips were between his knees and my shoulders were between his hands and my robed back was against the duvet. I felt it with my fingers. Not polyester.

Maybe it was the not-polyester, which reminded me of the polyester duvet in my own hotel room. Maybe it was his bare knees squeezing my hips. "Wait," I said, "can I—"

"No."

"But you didn't even hear—"

"I'm going to ask you a question."

"Okay, but—"

"Why are you here."

I shook my head.

"I told you."

"Barely."

"Now you tell me."

"Do you do this a lot?"

Do you do this a lot. His mouth twisted. "No, don't do that, you know better than that."

"Know better than—" I raised my head, shifted my weight, tried to sit up on the bed but already he had lowered his body onto mine, raised my hands above my head. Already he had secured both my hands with one of his own, squeezed those thick, promising fingers around my wrists.

"You *do* do this a lot, don't you."

He shook his head. "Stop. Asking. That question." He was six feet tall, six-two. One-seventy, one-eighty. I've never been good at estimating weights.

"Look," I said, trying to move my hands, "I think—"

"No," he said, "answer my question. Why are you here." His grip tightened.

"Why do you care."

"Tell me why you're here."

"Can I have some bourbon?"

"Tell me," he said, "why you're here."

"Please," I said, "may I *please* have some bourbon."

"No," he said.

"You didn't even think about it."

"I didn't."

"You're not going to let me off this bed," I said, "are you."

He put the hand that was not on my wrists against my neck, very lightly. "Answer," he said, "my question."

"I'm here," I said, "because my husband is a very nice man. I am very mean to my husband and my husband is very nice to me and I feel, therefore, like a monster." The blood in my neck was throbbing against his thumb. It was not an unpleasant sensation. "I feel like a monster," I said, "and this is his fault. Even thinking it's his fault, only a monster would think that. I am here because my husband loves me, even though I am a monster and therefore unlovable. I am here," I said, "because I hate myself. I am here because I want someone else to hate me, too. I am here to prove my monstrousness to myself and to my husband. I am here because I want someone else to see it. I want someone else to see, to confirm, my monstrousness, too." Something like that.

Silence. His lips fluttered, like he was trying not to smile.

"You don't like yourself very much."

I shook my head.

"And you don't want me to like you very much, either."

I shook my head again.

"I'm asking because girls get confused. Some girls, you have to tie their wrists, make the knot real firm, can't trust them like I trust you." I felt my breath in my throat. "You know, I'm stronger than you but I'm holding your two wrists with my one hand. You could break my grip. You could break my grip if you wanted to, only you don't want to." He moved his hand away from my neck, began untying, began opening my bathrobe. "But some girls, some girls get confused. Some girls don't know what they want. And then you have to tie their wrists up real tight even before you take your belt off, even though she should know, she should know you'd only ever use the leather end, you'd never use the buckle end. Sometimes, how she's moving against the knot you used on her wrist, you change your mind, you leave the belt on the floor. My belt, right now, just so you know, it's on this bed, it's right where I can reach it. With some girls, you're not even hitting her yet, and all of a sudden, just totally out of the blue, she starts looking scared. She starts saying, What are you doing, starts saying, Hold on a minute, starts saying, Wait I don't know about this, and so then you do have to hit her"—and here he slapped me—"not hard"—no, not hard, a sting, brief, and then the pleasure of the sting's absence—"just to get her to shut up but then she opens her mouth like she's going to scream," he shook his head, "so you have to put your other hand against her mouth and now her eyes are open wide and now you can tell that she's scared and so you put your knees on her thighs because she's starting to move too much, it's starting to seem like she might try to get up, get off the bed. You know," he said, "my knees aren't on your thighs because I know I can trust you. You can get off this bed anytime you want," he said, "only I know you won't. I know you won't because you're not going to get scared, are you. No, you're not going to start looking at me like *please*, like *don't*. Because when girls do that then you have to raise your hand again, because if a girl's going to be scared, well," he smiled, "you might as well scare her, you know, you might as well hit her," he raised his hand, "I mean you might as well really hit her, on the ribs maybe, just below the tits, some place that won't show when she puts her dress back on. But when a girl's confused," he shook his head, "you go to lower your hand," he slapped me again, harder this time, "and she closes her eyes and that," he shook his head, "well that ruins it. You have to untie the knot. You have to get off the bed. You have to tell her to leave. You have to let her go. Do you," he said, his hand resting on my throat, beginning to squeeze, "do you want me to let you go?"

"No," I said. "Don't worry," I said. "I won't," I said. "I won't close my eyes."

Los Angeles, 2012

The curtain rises on: my mother's kitchen; the curtain rises on: me, making myself a gin and tonic. It was early afternoon; I'd been in Los Angeles two days. This part is hard to talk about, I dislike doing it, for that reason I may, forgive me, attempt to be funny.

I drove back from San Francisco in the morning. I didn't shower. This was a Sunday. I found John and I sat him down and said, *I'm having an affair.* Of course it wasn't an affair it was a one-night stand, but I thought *affair* was smarter, as in more painful. *Smart* as in *to smart,* my words a hot needle, digging into John's palm. Then I waited. I waited for him to say he wanted a divorce. Instead he sat down on our couch and put his head in his hands. Instead he said, I love you. Instead he said, What about therapy.

That business about the hot needle, you know heat is also used to cauterize. Say *one-night stand,* offer the hope of *mistake* of *won't happen again,* inflict the first of many wounds, so much pain before the one that's fatal. No, not the first, for years I'd been poking at him, that was the problem. Hard to believe, but this was me trying to stop, this was me trying to be kind. After a fashion. *Affair*, though, deep but clean I thought, he'll want to walk away I thought, heat the knife, press it to the wound, stop the bleeding. Knife, needle, in moments of emotional extremity it's true, my metaphors become mixed.

What I didn't expect: John, on the couch, his head very recently in his hands, saying, What about therapy. And if the sight of him, I think I do not exaggerate if I use the word *devastated*, if this provoked pain it also provoked anger. At his weakness. Provoked also disgust. I was stuck with myself wasn't I, but here he was being given a chance to walk away and here he was squandering it.

Perhaps the conversation continued beyond my initial refusal. I mean my refusal to speak, so it was more of a monologue, John saying, Don't you love me, and Shouldn't we give ourselves a chance to fix this, and We were going to have a baby, and me not trusting myself to open my mouth. How animals, caught in a trap, will gnaw off their own limbs, maybe it was a little like that only I think the comparison gives me too much credit, it was John's limb and I was the one chewing, him saying, I still think we can make this work, him saying, Here, do you want this leg, too.

Anyway if the conversation did continue I don't

remember any of it, what I remember is saying, I'm going now, what I remember is calling a cab and going to the airport, what I remember is buying a ticket to Los Angeles at the airport and how expensive it was.

I hadn't called my parents ahead of time. I wasn't ready to answer questions, and questions are more easily ignored in person than on the phone. Besides which I didn't need to because the fact is that my parents are lovely people, really very nurturing. My father more notionally as in he'd love to be but mostly he isn't around, my mother sloppier the later it gets, but well-intentioned, both of them, and kind. Gentle with me, eager to care for me, my mother especially, traits as unforgivable in a parent as in a lover.

So they'd welcomed me in and allowed me to ignore their questions and now it was two days later, early afternoon, and I was in the kitchen making myself a gin and tonic. My whole body, I should mention, abuzz with fury. Drinking an attempt to calm down. Furious with myself because by the time I got to Los Angeles I'd realized, I wasn't stupid, that I'd done it all *wrong*.

The childhood fantasy of running away, we're all familiar, yes? Similar in many respects to the childhood fantasy of being allowed to witness one's own funeral, the difference is only in emphasis. The child who dreams of witnessing her own funeral dreams of being allowed to hear the unqualified praise that is due the dead; mere mention of her faults is, if only temporarily, if only publicly, banned. The child who dreams of running away knows that in so doing she provokes anger, that her action may in fact be an occasion for the dredging up and reexamination of wrongs committed. But what is this to her? Those wrongs, like the people she has wronged, lie in the past; she has given herself the chance to begin anew.

Of course there's a reason this fantasy belongs to childhood. Starting over is difficult and painful and the past isn't dead and buried it isn't even, etc. And the fact is that starting over becomes more so—difficult and painful I mean—the older one gets, for the older one gets the more numerous the ties to the life one wishes to leave behind, the more ties therefore to cut. The more ties therefore, later, if one is possessed of what is sometimes called a weak ego and what is sometimes called a conscience, to mend.

What I mean is I'd waited too long. If I'd changed my life after leaving graduate school. If I'd changed my life after moving to Lincoln. But I'd waited too long; I'd waited long enough that a change in my life provoked also a change in the lives of others, a violent and unwanted change that I would eventually, I was aware of this, I was not so wholly without feeling that I did not care about this, have to, I think the term is *deal with*.

Let me try to explain this another way. As a child, my interests, if you could call them that, were the highly regimented activities at which I immediately excelled. The fact that I'm one dissertation away from a PhD in English, this is at least in part because I read easily and early and because grown-ups, teachers especially, do love to compliment a little girl with a big book. If homework can be a hobby it was, throughout elementary and middle and high school, primary among mine. What I wanted was direction and praise for following it. As a child these were easy to find. As an adult I learned that the only people who seemed inclined to give out both were my professors, married men, almost all of them. But you can't marry your married professor. So instead I married John. John, who was so kind and so supportive and emotionally generous and a good listener, who was everything a liberated woman is supposed to want. But then there was no one to pat me on the head for making the right choice. There was only John, who was so kind. Who was so kind and who wanted me to have desires of my own. Really it was a mean trick that the only one I developed was the desire to leave him.

What I'm trying to say, the theorem that must be accepted as a premise if any of my behavior is ever to make any sense, is that I have been, that I continue to be, best at being a vessel for the desire of others. And that this has made me good at exactly two things, school and sex. Also that you're not supposed to use people as means to an end, you're only supposed to treat them as ends in and of themselves, a very smart and famous man by the name of Immanuel Kant says so. Only I did want to be used as a means, and mostly it made me miserable and was evil besides, and in an attempt to fix this fundamental problem with me as a person I'd used John as a means and that, not questions like What are you going to do for money, and How are you going to find a job, and Have you opened the e-mail from your manager in response to the e-mail in which you quit without notice, and Is it irony to quit without notice i.e. in a very inappropriate way when the job you're quitting is in HR, the fact that I'd used John, that was what was eventually going to bother me, when I allowed myself to feel things again.

But the time when I allowed myself to feel things again, that time was not now. Now was early afternoon and I was fixing myself a gin and tonic and watching YouTube videos. In the spirit of Well certainly there must be people who are even more miserable and evil than me, the search terms I was using included the word *violent* and also the word *marriage*.

What I found first was a scene from Robert Altman's 1973 film *The Long Goodbye*. This was one-and-a-half gin and tonics later. In the scene, a gangster breaks a Coke bottle across his girlfriend's face. The attack is unprovoked. The girlfriend is wearing a peach-colored dress made of some gauze-like material, chiffon, possibly. The dress has modified bell sleeves that cinch at the wrist and are finished with ruffles. It has what appears to be a natural waist, likely elastic, though this is impossible to determine with any certainty because the waist is partially concealed by a loose, slightly asymmetrical panel that falls on top of and is constructed of the same material as the body of the dress. The panel floats on the left side to just below, and on the right side to just above, the elbow. The girlfriend's name is Jo Ann Eggenweiler and she is played by an actress named Jo Ann Brody. Not an actress, a waitress who served Altman and two members of his cast during a break in the shooting of the only scene in which she appears. Onscreen, Jo Ann is mostly silent. She and her gangster boyfriend, Marty, are in Philip Marlowe's apartment. Philip Marlowe is played by Elliott Gould. She sits, impassive, while Marty tells her how beautiful she is, how much he loves her. "I sleep with a lot of girls," he says, "but I make love to you. Right?" She nods. A few moments later, he breaks the Coke bottle across her face. She screams. As the gangster's henchmen hustle her off-screen, she utters two words: "Oh god!" "Now, that's someone I love," the gangster says to Marlowe. "And you I don't even like."

What I found next was a forty-five-minute video labeled "Norman Mailer Documentary Interview

Outtake." The still above the link was of a slim woman, white-haired, in a skirt suit, cream-colored, possibly linen. She was sitting in a leather armchair; beside her, a wooden side table held a bucket of ice, a crystal decanter partially filled with brown liquid, and a square glass, it too partially filled with liquid, though of a lighter brown color, the color of whiskey or bourbon diluted by ice. Her left hand was at her neck, two fingers touching a string of pearls. I clicked. As the video buffered, I read the description: "Outtake from *Mailer: An American Life* (2005). Raw footage, interview subject unknown." The first comment below was irate: "who is this woman is and why did they interviewed her?? skimmed whole video (to long)) and she doesnt seem to kno anything about mailer just complains about her husband dont watch if ur interested in mailer hes is a great american writer (and check out his movies to!!) this woman is just some old bitch!!!" There was a reply immediately below from the same commenter. "In case you're wondering I do know how to spell and also all the rules of grammar, in fact I'm very well read, I was just too infuriated to care. Lol. :)" In the fourteen days since the video had been posted, one hundred and twelve people had watched it. Seventy had given it a thumbs-down. The video was done buffering.

"Tell me," a voice offscreen said, "about the party."

"Yes," the woman onscreen said, "there was a party.

It was Norman Mailer's party. It was 1960 and I was dating a man named Bill and Bill said Norman Mailer was throwing a party and we were invited." She was wearing coral-colored lipstick on slim, wrinkled lips. Lipstick the color of Florida, the color of retirement and open-toed orthopedic sandals and parchment-thin skin, cool and dry in the air-conditioning. "I put on a silk sheath dress," she said, "peach-colored with flowers embroidered in bronze and cream thread. Bill said Norman was running for mayor." Her right ankle was crossed over her left. With her right thumb and index finger, she turned the glass in a circle on its coaster. "Bill said, Everyone important is going to be there. Bill said, George Plimpton is going to be there, and I said, Does George like a girl in gloves?"

"What happened," a voice offscreen said, "at the party?"

"It was a joke," the woman onscreen said. No acknowledgment of the question, not even a dismissive wave. "It was a joke but also I didn't know who George Plimpton was, only that I was supposed to be impressed with him. Bill laughed. I barely knew who Norman was. I brought my gloves, just in case. The dress was decorated, at the waist, with a flat little bow, also pink, and the flowers were abstracted. Very chic, very Rothko." She smiled. "That's what I thought. Actually they looked like eggs from a distance. Like single eggs, mid-fry." She turned her head to cough.

"When you got—"

"My hair was straight as a board and I'd spent twenty minutes, before the party, curling the ends under. George Plimpton did end up being there, though he was gone by the time it happened."

"Yes, if you could—"

"With the ends curled under my hair just grazed the tops of my shoulders. It was auburn then, my hair was"—the woman touched her soft white bun— "in the right light. Bill knew Norman," she continued, "because he'd been at Rinehart when *The Naked and the Dead* came out. He'd been the novel's copy editor, which mostly meant changing all the *fuck*s to *fug*s and all the *fucking*s to *fugging*s and also getting yelled at by Norman. Every time he saw a typo in the proofs, Norman would call Bill up and start yelling. No use explaining to Norman that it was the typesetter's fault. Years passed"—she took a sip from the glass—"and then they ran into each other again, at a party in the Village, or maybe it was in fact a *Village Voice* party, I forget. Norman was gesticulating and he bumped Bill's hand and Bill said, Watch your *fugging* hands, prick, and Norman turned, his mouth a kind of snarl—Bill always made this funny face when he told the story—and said, Who the *fuck* are you, and Bill said, It's *fug*, Mr. Mailer, I'm afraid we can't print *fuck*, and Norman said, Where do I know that— And then he was laughing and his arms were around Bill's torso, wrestling him into a bear hug.

Bill's drink got all over Norman's shirt but Norman wasn't angry, took off his shirt, good-natured, went and got him another drink. Anyway, after that, Norman started inviting Bill to parties—"

"Speaking of parties, if we could—"

"—calling him from the phone booth outside the Fire Spot or the Open Door." She spoke a bit louder, was the only indication that she'd been aware of the interruption. "And sometimes when Norman called I was with Bill and then we went together. This was fifty-eight or fifty-nine. At first Norman liked when I showed up with Bill. I was twenty in fifty-eight, long legs and high breasts, a little bitty waist cinched in between. I was"—her eyes were aimed at a spot to the left of the camera and here they narrowed—"gorgeous though I suppose it's hard to tell now, back then a young man would have at least pretended to—"

"I'm sorry, of course, it's only with our schedule, I'm sure you understand, Ms.—"

"Never mind, never mind," one hand waving. "What was I—right, I was going to say that I was taller than Norman in stocking feet, which is true. He was a short man. I towered over him in heels. I think he thought I was a WASP, which I wasn't, though my family did live in Connecticut and it was true that I didn't own a pair of dungarees"—eyes narrowing—"I mean *jeans*. My father worked fixing cars, wore coveralls at the shop and dungarees at home, but my mother dressed me like the little girls who lived in the houses she cleaned, darling boat-necked numbers with pleated skirts, pinafores, smock fronts. Not a closetful but two or three that she let out at the waist when I grew wider and at the hem when I grew longer. My mother was a good seamstress, she added bows at the back when the fashions changed, sewed in Peter Pan collars. It was my mother who bought me my first pair of gloves, told me a lady always wears gloves to drinks, to dinner. Never leave the house after four o'clock without your gloves, she told me. White gloves, and don't let them get dirty. My mother was Italian, southern, dark, but my father was fair and I was too, didn't look—the word then was *ethnic*. Thirteen or fourteen years old, I remember being in the bathroom with my mother, my mother dusting my cheeks with white powder, telling me to stay out of the sun. I played with the girls whose houses my mother cleaned, indoor games only. At least until I was eleven or twelve. Then it became unseemly." She cleared her throat. "Once, at P.J. Clarke's he—Norman—came up from behind and grabbed me not quite around the waist. I was wearing a mauve skirt that hit at mid-calf, tight around the hips, and a white blouse, high-necked, cap sleeves trimmed with lace, buttons down the back. In my ear he said, What would your daddy say if he could see you now, and then he laughed. Where he got the idea that my family—I mean I don't

know who, exactly, he thought my daddy was, but—
Maybe he also kissed my neck but his lips were so
close to my ear it could have been accidental, just"—
she flicked an invisible piece of lint from her skirt—
"damp brushing." She pursed her lips. "I could look
rich, that's true, or rich enough. When I say, *At
first Norman liked when I showed up,* I mean at first I
did. Then Bill came out of the bathroom and said,
Now, Norman, you know that's my girl, and Norman pinched my ass, released me, winked. Winked
at Bill, I mean. Can you hear the smile in Bill's voice?
He wanted to be hip, Norman did, and that was the
problem, that was what made him so square. When I
say, *I barely knew who Norman was,* I mean I knew him
as a creep. I mean I played dumb. I was young and
pretty and I hadn't gone to college and I didn't have
artistic ambitions, wasn't an actress or a painter or
a poet, it was easy enough. The man who wrote the
bestsellers, who went on television, who won prizes,
accolades, the man of whom my boyfriend stood in
awe. That man. Didn't know him"—these words less
said than spit—"didn't want to."

Now there was a pause. On the screen, the woman
sipped from her drink. She fingered the pearls of her
necklace. I watched the clasp move, clockwise, from
the nape of her neck to the base of her throat, then
back around to the nape. Two circuits in, the sound
of throat clearing from offscreen. "You were talking
about"—a cough—"if we could maybe get back to—"

"The party, right. It was a birthday party. Roger somebody or other. Of course Bill acknowledged Norman had his eccentricities. Sure he was a little free with his hands, cheated on his wife, liked his bourbon, liked his dope, who didn't. I liked my bourbon, didn't I? Sure I did." She raised her glass, took another sip, a longer sip, swallowed hard. "If you're rich it's not called getting drunk, it's called having a good time. Norman had grown up poor but now he was rich and he was having a hell of a time. His last two novels, sure they'd been panned but that was because the press was against him, he was too radical, they were afraid of him but what the hell, who cared, because Norman could make your party, that's what everybody said. He'd show up with Adele, two or three friends, drunk already, on his third or fourth party of the night, slugging from a fifth of whiskey, and he'd find the prettiest girl in the room and start a staring contest with her. Find a big guy and start thumb wrestling with him. Find a bigger guy and start head-butting him. I remember the skulls coming together, crashing, once"—she clenched her hands into fists, knocked her knuckles together—"twice, three times, four times, until someone fell down. Pick the guy up, pick himself up, start the game over. He'd clear out the living room, get down on the carpet, play bongos with his feet while waxing lyrical about, oh, marijuana or jazz or the hipster or Western literature and his place in it.

The orgy as existential act. Was he better or worse than Bill Styron, than Jim Jones, than Scott Fitzgerald. Bill thumb wrestled him at a party once and the next day he couldn't hold a pencil." She laughed. "Once, at a party, Norman put on a record—we were back at his place, an apartment on the East Side—and it wasn't music, it was Norman talking. Norman mid-monologue in this fake Texas accent. Someone giggled. I turned to the girl next to me and I started to say—and Norman turned to me and he said, *Shut the* fuck *up*."

On the screen the woman leaned forward. "If anyone else were doing it, man, what a drag. But Norman, well, he was *brilliant*, he was a *genius*"—the veins on her neck visible—"you could listen to him talk all night and boy sometimes that was exactly what you did. Bill would tell me all about it on those nights when he went out to see Norman and I stayed in. He'd come home at four, high or stoned or both, puffed up with Norman, Norman, Norman. Sometimes I wondered that wasn't the name he cried out when we were fucking." I flinched. I think the camera operator did too, because the picture sort of wiggled. "Those nights he'd paw at me and I'd roll over so my back was to him. Some of us, I'd say, have to get up in the morning. And that was true, hell, never mind me, Bill had a job to get to too, but mostly I didn't want Bill to touch me with the stench of Norman on him. Sometimes I turned my back, shook my head, said, Come on, Bill, and still he flipped me so I was flat on my back, pinned my shoulders. Never *no*, couldn't quite figure out how to say that." Another kind of laugh, mirthless. "And anyway, Bill couldn't hold his liquor and the fight would tire him out and so it was only ever a few minutes. Usually he'd fall asleep with one hand stuck in my panties, the struggle to remove them having proven too exhausting, his dick only half hard." Every word carefully enunciated. "How he thought he was going to get it in." She shook her head, settled back into her chair. Hint of a smile. "Anyway, that's how it usually went, easy enough, once he was snoring, to roll out from under him, take a quarter Seconal, or half, be up by seven, powder under the eyes to cover the circles."

She shook her head again, recrossed her legs. A pause, but this time there was nothing from off-screen. "I didn't want to go to the party but by then I'd stayed home too many nights and this wasn't just any party it was a birthday party and not only a birthday party but also somehow connected to Norman's mayoral campaign. He launched it, two days later, on Mike Wallace's television show. Wallace didn't even ask him about the stabbing, I guess he hadn't heard the news. I read, after, that Norman invited everyone he could find, the grungier the better, druggies and drunks, punks and hustlers, his *constituents* he called them, said they would be the ones to vote for him, the ones he intended to represent. Like they were registered. I'll say this, he was a good salesman. He had a nose for—scandal, maybe, or opportunity. Press. Later I read that Norman liked to surround himself with sycophants, you know, second-raters, has-beens, never-would-bes. They meant the boxers and the bullfighters, the nobody knockabouts he picked up in bars, guys who could match him drink for drink, punch for punch, and that wasn't—I mean Bill was, like I said, a lightweight, but reading *sycophants*, reading *second-raters*, well, I thought of Bill. He was the very first person who came to mind." She was silent for a moment, one hand touching the pearls of her necklace, the beads shifting beneath her fingers.

"It was close to midnight when we got there." Relaxed in her armchair, her body turned away from the camera, one hand on the pearls, the other cradling the glass, almost empty. "I'd dragged my feet, done my hair and then brushed it out and then done it again, ordered two martinis at dinner, some kind of dessert liqueur. Plus the apartment was on the Upper West Side, so it took a while to get there on the IRT." The beads of the rosary, that's what the pearls reminded me of. "It was a big place, but glum, the walls dark green, and so packed with people, still, that to get to the bar you had to push your way through the crowd. I sent Bill for drinks and fought my way to the bathroom, crumbs and ashes on the carpet, sweet smoke in the air, an elbow in the ribs, a hand on my ass. A woman, a stranger, opened the door as I was trying the handle. She was tall, taller than me, and blond, her blunt bangs gone stringy, clinging, sweat-smeared, to her forehead. The stranger pushed past me and then I was face-to-face with Adele. Her name's gone now, the stranger's, but I must have known it at some point because I can remember hearing, later, that the fight started because she'd been in the bathroom with Adele, the implication being that they were"—the woman's lip curled—"you know, making it, what you would call *hooking up*. She looked old, Adele did. I remember thinking she looked old. And that wasn't just the cruelty of my youth"—smiling now, the lines that framed the corners of her face deepening—"she had aged in the six months since I'd last seen her, her eyes were small and beady, red-rimmed, swollen. I mean it was obvious what they'd been, what Adele had been doing, she'd been *crying*, that other rumor," the woman scoffed, lifted her left hand from her neck so she could wave it dismissively. "Clumps of mascara in her eyelashes and black smudges on her cheekbones. She looked, for a second, less startled than afraid. Just for a moment. Then she composed herself, she smiled, and she did this—this sort of shimmy—and she said, You haven't seen Norman, have you? I shook my head. She frowned, drained her martini glass, brought a hand to her chest, giggled. I suppose, she said, I shall have to track him down myself. Her voice rose as she pronounced *myself,* rose and caught. She handed me her empty glass, winked, smoothed her dress. Husbands, she said, rolling her eyes. Her cheeks were puffy and I saw, as she turned, disappeared into the crowd"—the woman's voice was low now—"she was wearing this black velvet dress, the back cut low in a V, and as she turned I saw that above the V, the skin of her back was blushing this deep, painful-looking red. Anxiety, maybe. Embarrassment. I read, later, that the kids, two girls, were upstairs the whole time."

The woman cleared her throat. "You know we'd all heard the rumors. The arrest in Provincetown after he'd tried to hail a cop car as if it were a cab. A drunk and disorderly charge after a dispute at some bar. The rumors and then the excuses, didn't we know how the cops hated Norman, the real story was about a cabaret license, the cops were fascists anyway, there was no trusting them. And look"—the woman on the screen sighed—"the police *did* deny cabaret licenses arbitrarily, especially to black musicians, to black singers, and Norman *was* involved in a protest, helped circulate a petition, but also, *separately*, he got too drunk at a bar and the police were called and he was charged with a drunk and disorderly. And it's not like that was the only time—I mean there were also those whispers about Adele's makeup not quite covering up a black eye, a split lip, a bruise on the neck or the shoulder or the arm. The temper, the affairs. He'd shown up drunk to a lecture

111

at Princeton, no it was Brown. He'd flown into a rage and hit his sister across the face, or was it his mother, was it his mistress. Not that I'd"—she paused, leaned toward the camera—"not that I'd ever seen anything, anything definitive. Later it turned out"—she leaned back—"or anyway I read that he'd spent that very afternoon, the afternoon of the party, drunk with a friend at an actress's apartment, in the actress's bedroom, the friend passed out and the actress trying to fend Norman off, Norman refusing to leave until the actress threatened to call the police. Anyway, that's what I read."

The woman uncrossed and recrossed her legs. She smoothed out her skirt, leaned back in her chair. "Adele provoked him. That was the line. Also that she had affairs of her own, and that *is* true. And not just with men, with women, threesomes. Once, at a party, she took off all her clothes and tried to start an orgy. She pulled another girl's hair, tried to scratch her face, and this was all in public, on the sand dunes out in Provincetown, dozens of witnesses. And sure it was true but the, the *shit* she got for it and the shit he didn't." She shook her head. "Adele was known for"—lips pursed—"for her *outsized appetites,* for her *lingerie,* all Frederick's of Hollywood, to hear the gossips tell it that woman had never owned a pair of cotton panties in her life, she was a *sexual exotic.* You'll find that in the biographies, that exact phrase, *sexual exotic.* I know, I've read them. You'll find that Adele's mother was Spanish and her father was a *Peruvian Indian* and that she herself was born in Cuba. You'll find that she was a painter, too, a talented one, but that's introductory material, it always gets dropped quickly. Well"—she cleared her throat—"I've read one biography and a big chunk of another. Not that Norman wouldn't hit a white woman, he beat his fourth wife up at least once, and not in private, and she was a blonde, she was paler than me. But the fact that she wasn't white, that Adele wasn't, I think it made it easier. Not for Norman to do it, but for the rest of them. For the rest of us." She drank down what remained in her glass in one long swallow. "For me," she said. "For me to do nothing. I hadn't inherited my mother's, her *carnagione*, her complexion, her skin tone, but I had inherited her shame about it. And I think I thought that if I said something everyone would notice that I didn't belong. That I didn't belong, either. And anyway the scales were always going to be tipped in Norman's favor. I mean, it's Norman Mailer, public intellectual, on one side, and on the other"—she waved her hand—"some bitch. Some bitch Norman happens to have married. Who even remembers the *names* of all of his wives, never mind the fights, the affairs, the middle-of-the-night— I mean I don't. But the way they talked about her, before. The way they talk about her even now, in the biographies. I do think it was easier. To look away. To say she dragged her girlfriend into the bathroom to fuck, Adele never could get enough, didn't we all *know* that, look at her *mouth,* look how it's painted red, look at the dresses she wears, look how they're cut. It was never the race thing outright, they always covered the race thing with the sex thing. Spread the stories around, said see, said she got what she deserved, no more, no less."

She paused a moment, raised the glass to her lips, realized it was empty, lowered it. "Anyway. I was closing the door to the bathroom when I saw Adele bend to pick up the pieces of a canapé, a filo dough something-or-other, that someone had ground into the carpet. She looked around for a minute, her head swiveling, searching for a trash can I guess, and then her head dipped and she shrugged and she dropped the pieces back on the floor and walked away."

Another pause, and then her eyes narrowed. "I'm guessing you want to know about the famous people, right? So many famous people there that night, but I'm afraid I'm going to have to disappoint you"—a little smile here—"because by this time George was gone. He hadn't brought his rich friends and Norman had hit him in the head with a rolled-up newspaper and so he'd left. Lillian was gone and Dwight was gone or else they'd never been there. Barney Rosset was gone and Allen Ginsberg was gone and so was Delmore Schwartz. I read all those names later and anyway they would have meant nothing to me at the time. It was three-thirty in the morning, and then it was four. Shel was gone, too. Someone had put a cigarette out on the dark green wall. Meat underfoot. The room wasn't spinning but it wasn't staying steady, either. I sat down on a couch, put my head between my knees. Next to me two boys in suits were talking about Norman. Norman was outside, in the street, challenging passersby to boxing matches. He was so original, Norman was. Not only his prose but the way he lived. *Uncompromising*. A rejection of the editorial impulse, in life as in art. The human mask was *itself* an editorial impulse! Norman's acceptance—no, his *embrace* of man's animal nature. Violence as natural and therefore erotic, the erotic defined as all that has been prohibited by square society, including, of course, sex and death and fistfights." Her head had been moving back and forth as she described the boys' conversation but now it stopped. "Norman had a knife, one of the boys said. Norman was interested in the question of evil. Like Dostoevsky, one of the boys said. Yes, like Dostoevsky. This is what I remember. Or maybe I'm adding the dialogue later. The boys went back and forth. I held my head."

Here she paused. Silence. Silence for so long I thought maybe the sound had cut out, raised the volume on my computer, paused and unpaused the video, waited. Then shuffling from the other side of the camera, a throat clearing, a voice. "Are you," the voice began, "can I—"

"Give me," the woman said, holding up a hand, "a minute. Just give me a minute." Her other hand, its grip tightening on the empty glass. Then she said, "We were downstairs when it happened. Bill found me and helped me up and made me drink water with just a little bourbon in it and we took the elevator down. I didn't actually see it. Just to be clear. I didn't hear a scream or a crash, just the chatter in the lobby, a group had gathered, it was almost December and cold, we were all dreading walking to the subway, trying to hail a cab"—her hand was moving—"I remember honking outside, the sound of brakes. Then the elevator opened and a black man stepped out and he was holding Adele. Her dress was torn but it was dark and because the dress was black velvet it took a second to see the blood, to see that she was bleeding. Someone took her hand. Someone called an ambulance." Here the woman closed her eyes. And when she spoke she spoke softly but clearly and she kept her eyes closed. "It seems," she said, "important to mention. The fact that the man who helped Adele was black. I was going to say of course he was, of course the one black man left at this party was the only one who would help"—she paused—"because of course he was an outsider, too, or maybe he had less to lose"—she paused again—"but it all sounds wrong, how it comes out. Like I'm letting us off the hook. Or underestimating the risk he took. Or turning him into," she sighed. "Adele wrote a memoir, years later, and she called him, the man who helped her, her *dark angel*. Like he wasn't a person at all, with his own family, his own problems, someone who just happened, who had the decency—" Another sigh. "Like he was some supernatural manifestation. Like he was just for her. I know she meant it kindly. Still." Her eyes snapped back open. "Still it seems important to note. The black man, helping her downstairs. All the white people in the lobby, me included, doing nothing. Him gone before we could talk to him or maybe it was us not talking to him and him leaving. I remember it being very silent and then someone, a man, said, She fell on some broken glass, and a different voice, also male, said, You fell on some broken glass, Adele, didn't you, silence, Didn't you, silence, Didn't you, and then something that must have been assent. I was squeezing Bill's hand hard, too hard, and he said, Ow, and when I didn't let go he said, Honey, that hurts. I didn't"—she twisted her mouth—"leave him then, of course I didn't. No, I saw Adele bleeding and I heard my boyfriend say, Ow, and Honey that hurts, and I think we should go, and I let him lead me out of the lobby and onto the sidewalk."

The woman poured herself another splash of bourbon. The bottle was maybe a third full now. "We walked home," she said. "I wouldn't get into a cab with Bill, wouldn't go down the subway stairs with him, so we walked, a hundred blocks, more. Freezing, my breath white in the air and I couldn't feel the cold. All my thoughts were about walking, how to do it. Thinking heel toe, heel toe, heel toe. Thinking now right, now left, now right, now left. Bill pulled his hand out of my hand and after that I wouldn't touch him. For the first twenty blocks I wouldn't speak to him. He said, Honey, come here, and Baby, it's going to be okay, and Look, I don't know what happened, but we're fine, we're going to be fine"—she was speaking more quickly now—"and Man, what a party. I took my heels off, my stocking feet were on the cracked concrete now, and when he tried to put his arms around me I pushed him away, pushed my heels—my shoes had these sharp heels and I pushed them into his chest. He made a sound, a grunt. The noise scared me, I don't know why but it scared me, and I screamed. Somewhere around block thirty he said, Okay, I give up, what do you think happened, and I stopped and turned toward him and he stopped and turned toward me and I spit in his face. And then we kept walking. At some point I said, Bill, your friend Norman stabbed his wife. And he said, quickly, he said, Did you see a knife, and She said she fell on broken glass, you must have heard that, and I said, No, I heard someone tell her to say that. I said, Bill, if she dies, your friend Norman will have killed her and he will be a murderer, I said, You will be friends with a murderer how do you feel about that, and Bill said nothing. By the end I couldn't feel my feet. Finally I stopped and tried to put my heels back on but I couldn't force my toes in so I took my gloves off, white gloves, spotless, elbow-length, and I jammed them onto my feet. I left my shoes on the sidewalk. I shoved my hands into the pockets of my coat and I walked the last few blocks like that."

She exhaled and sipped from her glass and I exhaled too, I hadn't known I'd been holding my breath. "Bill said it one more time, quietly. We were inside our building, walking up the stairs, him in front and me trailing, the gloves on my feet flapping and folding and tripping me up, and because he was in front of me I only barely caught it, he mumbled it under his breath, he said, You don't know what happened. And then he was turning the lock in the key of our apartment and we were walking in."

I paused the video. I'd finished my gin and tonic, my second I think, no, it had to have been my third, and I walked to the liquor cabinet to make myself another, stopped, went over to the sink, filled my glass with water and drank it down, filled the glass again. I stood there for a minute, my back against the sink, sipping and thinking. Thinking, Adele, you were such a good girl. Thinking, No one imagined. No one could have imagined what a good girl you would be.

I sat back down, clicked the video. "I didn't go to sleep that night," the woman said. "Bill went straight to the bedroom but I wasn't tired and it was morning already anyway, past six. I poured myself a glass of bourbon, a tall glass, no ice, and drew myself a bath, waited for the feeling to return to my feet, to the tips of my fingers, to the end of my nose. Then I put on a clean white blouse, brushed my hair, tied it back, slipped on low heels. Bill was lying on top of the sheets, fully clothed. He was snoring. I grabbed gloves, gray cashmere. There was a small hole between the fourth and fifth fingers of the left hand. I remember noticing the hole. I remember thinking, I'll have to mend these. I crossed the street and bought a pack of cigarettes and a cup of coffee at the newsstand. I bought copies of the *Times,* the *Daily News,* and the *Post.* In the apartment I read each cover to cover. Not that I expected to find anything, the papers would have already gone to press, just I wanted—now that the sun was up and it wasn't so cold and outside I'd seen a family, father in a suit and coat and hat and mother in gloves and children in patent leather, it seemed possible I'd gotten carried away, let my emotions get the— But then I remembered the father's grip on the mother's wrist, hadn't it seemed too firm, shouldn't they have been holding hands, not— Maybe I was becoming hysterical, women are prone to hysterics after all, this is a well-known fact." She took a breath. "After I read the papers cover to cover I threw them away. Then I found a pair of scissors and cut up the gloves I'd worn the night before, cut them up until they were just small squares of fabric. They were useless now that they were no longer white. I threw the small squares of fabric away. I sat on the couch and smoked. By the time Bill woke up I'd finished the pack."

The woman cleared her throat. "I bought the papers on Monday, too, but there wasn't anything until Tuesday. Buried halfway through the *Times*, a column and a half, barely, plus a half-column-sized picture of Norman. It did make the front page of the *Daily News*. I remember the headline. Wife Stabbed, Novelist Held. I remember it specifically because I read later that Adele's father was a typesetter at the *Daily News*, that that's how he found out."

She took a sip from her drink. "Bill apologized to me later. And he broke with Norman. Or he said he did. There were nights, later, nights when I wondered, when he didn't come home, or came home drunk, nights when I lay, still, waiting, eyes open in the dark."

She paused. Raised the glass then lowered it. "Years passed," she said. "Years passed, as they do, and Bill and I got married." She laughed. "Got married. I want to say that if he hadn't apologized, if he hadn't stopped seeing Norman, I wouldn't—but I can't because that's not how it happened. Bill was a copy editor, then he was an assistant editor, then he was an editor, a senior editor, editor in chief. I was a secretary at an ad agency and then I was an assistant copywriter and then for a long time I was a full copywriter and then I was head copywriter and I had my own office. No kids. Bill wanted them and I didn't care one way or the other but it just never happened. We kept trying, a year, two years, three, and then we stopped trying and then Bill got a twenty-two-year-old pregnant, so I guess the problem was me. There was a quickie divorce, out of state, and then I went back to my office."

The woman shifted in her seat. "I wasn't," she said, "you know, I wasn't going to do this interview. And then last week, Thursday, I got the paper. The *Times*. And I read, I was eating my half a grapefruit, drinking my coffee, and I read that the man who hired me, who promoted me, who gave me my office, was a—" She paused. "Was a rapist. That's what the women say. Four of them. His assistants, assistants I remember, young girls, bright girls. That on business trips he told them to come to his hotel room and that in the hotel room he poured them drinks. That they said no but that it didn't matter, he didn't listen. The same story, with slight variations. One of them had bruises. One of them, a different one, went to the police, but it was a couple days later, she'd taken a shower. The detective she talked to said after seventy-two hours there wouldn't be any evidence left, told her to go home. I read this and thought, I was older when these assistants were hired. I thought, He never tried anything with me. I tried to remember, were there times when he called his assistant into his office, kept the door closed too long. When he asked his assistant to stay late. But I couldn't remember. Couldn't remember anything I would swear to.

"You know, Adele stuck to the story about falling on glass for the first few days, and then she changed her story and said Norman stabbed her and then, then"—the woman was pointing a finger—"then she changed it back. The grand jury indicted him anyway." The woman smiled. "Indicted him even though she said she was too drunk to remember what happened, that she and her husband were 'perfectly happy together.'" The woman made air quotes with one hand. "And good for them." She laughed. "He ended up pleading out, third-degree assault they called it, gave him five years' probation. He spent a couple weeks in Bellevue, this was before the indictment, but she wouldn't sign off on shock therapy. Of course she was trying to protect herself but then everyone blamed her anyway. Norman's mother, his friends, the entire quote-unquote literary establishment. They didn't divorce, not officially, until sixty-two. I remember knowing this—reading it, or maybe someone told me, you know how gossip gets around—and thinking I should look her up and say something, something like *I'm sorry*. It's too late now, of course. I never spoke to her again. Really," she said, "what I've always wondered is whether they got the blood out of that dress. It was a lovely dress, scoop-necked with a plunging back, long and fitted but not tight, like liquid, skimming the surface of her body, and probably ruined, what with it being velvet and velvet being so hard to wash, so hard to mend, at least if you're trying to do it properly, if you're trying to do it without leaving a seam." The woman sighed. "I think that's all I have to say."

"Do you want—"

"I think," she said firmly, "that is all I have to say." The last twelve seconds of the video were silent, the woman sitting in her chair, fingering her pearl necklace.

I was still at the kitchen table when my mother came home. For the past hour I'd been trying to figure out the woman's name. *Advertising* plus *executive* plus *rape* had returned some promising results, but it was hard enough to find a list of current employees, never mind headshots. Plus almost certainly she was retired. Possibly she was dead.

My mother was carrying a jade plant and three bouquets, three honest-to-goodness riots of color: orange birds-of-paradise and pink peonies and white anemones, their pistils blue-black and their petals so thin and pale they were almost translucent. "Sweetheart," she said, turning on a light, "it's so dark in here." The names of the flowers coming, by habit, unbidden, unbidden, too, the names of their parts. Though *pistil* seems too violent a term for eggs and an ovary and in fact I prefer to call this bit, conscious of the error and of my mother's chagrin, the flower's *nipple*. She opened a cabinet, pulled out two vases, fished scissors out of a drawer, turned on the faucet. One vase for the table in the kitchen, one vase for the table in the living room, the ratio of orange to pink to white in each would, I knew, be varied so that their symmetry would seem neither wholly accidental nor exactly planned. In front of my mother, on the kitchen counter, on the window-sill, philodendrons and spider plants, an English ivy, overgrown, a blooming bromeliad. I closed my computer. The plants I don't mind so much. "Hi, Mom." She trimmed the stems under the running water. "Productive day, sweetheart?" I shrugged. She takes good care of the plants, never seen one brown on her watch, never seen one die, and if they're not dying there's only so much space, only so many she can buy. "Leads on any jobs?" I shrugged again. It's the flowers I hate, fresh bunches almost every day, tossed, fine, *composted*, before any hint of wilt, like bright blooms aren't a luxury, like they're some kind of *need*. When we argue about the flowers, the arguments I make are about waste and about money, valid arguments both. Though in fact what I hate about the flowers is that they are, for my mother, a source of pleasure, that my mother believes in allowing herself pleasure, in indulging her various material desires. What I hate about the flowers is that they are an example of the many ways in which my mother extends her kindness also to herself.

"You'll never guess," my mother said, "who I ran into today," no pause, "you remember Esther? From elementary school? You sat next to her in the fourth grade, I think, or maybe it was fifth. Anyway, I ran into her mother at the farmers' market"—she was putting the flowers into vases now, mixing the birds-of-paradise with the peonies with the anemones— "you remember her, Marcia? Well, Marcia told me that Esther's a junior account executive at, wait"— she put a hand to her forehead—"let me think, it was either CAA or William Morris, one of those big entertainment companies, agencies they call them." "Mom, I know they—" "Anyway, Esther's looking for an assistant and I said you were back in town and that you were looking for a job and she gave me Esther's business card, the name of the company will be on the business card, I'm sure it's either William Morris or CAA, if you look in my purse it's in the little zipper pocket right at the top. Anyway, you should give her a call. That's what Marcia said, Marcia said that you should give Esther a call, that she would tell Esther that we ran into each other and that you were back in town and that she should expect to hear from you. I'm sure it's not much money but, you know, it could be a real kind of *start*, and if you want a new career you'll *have* to start at the bottom, and most people apparently start in the mailroom so this would already be a leg up—"

"Mom," I said, "I'm not even sure how long I'm going to be in Los Angeles."

My mother turned away from the sink. "Well that doesn't mean you shouldn't give yourself options. You might really like the job, maybe that—"

"Mom," I said, standing, tucking my computer under my arm, "I think I'm going to take a nap."

My mother frowned. "Are you feeling okay? Do you want me to make you some tea?"

"I'm fine, Mom. I'm just tired."

"Maybe some tea and a slice of toast? I could make you cinnamon toast, you used to—"

"Mom, I mean, *thank* you, but I'm not hungry, I'm *tired*. I'll be fine if I can just get—"

"It's just that you slept in this morning and if you're feeling sick we should get some food in you, maybe some vitamin C, too, here, I'll open one of those Emergen-Cs. Those'll knock out a cold in no time, especially if you catch it early, and I know I have some in the pantry, give me a second and I'll—"

"Mom." I was raising my voice, which I knew my mother would notice and which I suspected she would remember and hold against me but in a way that would make it seem as if she were not holding it against me, as if she were only being observant, as if she were only worried about me, about how I was holding up, this was, after all, *such* a stressful time. "Mom," I said, "I just need to rest. Give me an hour.

Just give me an hour. We can talk about Esther in an hour."

My mother abandoned her flowers, moved toward me, put her hands on my shoulders, her eyebrows furrowed, her lips pursed, she looked, genuinely—I bowed my head to avoid it, this most genuine look of affection pocked with pain. "Honey," she said, "look, honey, I know that this is—wait, honey, let me get this out." Her grip tightened. "I know this is—well actually I don't *know* much of *any*thing because you won't *tell* us what happened"—her voice sharpening— "but I know this *must*"—softening again—"I know this *must* be so hard, just so *hard* for you right now, and I want you to know that if you *need* anything, if you—now wait, don't shake your head yet, you don't know yet, you don't *know*. You might need something, and if you, if you *do* need anything, now, or maybe later, if you need *any*thing, your dad and me, we're here for you, you know that right?" Pause. "You *know* that, right?" Small nod. "And if you're worried—I mean I know you must be worried about a lot of things, I don't know exactly *what* because you won't—but, look, I want you to know that of course we loved John, me and your dad, of *course* we did, from the moment we *met* him he was just so *nice*, nice to you, *so* nice to me, not like—but I, *we*, we want you to know that we love John, but you're our *daughter* and you come first, whatever happens, whatever happened, whoever—whether it's your fault or—we just want you to know that you always come first, okay? So, you know, if you're worried that we—just know we love you and that you can come to us, okay? If you need anything?" The heat of my mother's body, her standing so close to me, I could feel it, also the smell of her deodorant mingling with the smell of her body wash mingling with the smell of her laundry detergent. Hot outside, must have been. If I looked up, I was sure that if I looked up, I would have been able to see a light sheen of sweat on my mother's upper lip. "Come here, baby." My mother wrapped her arms around my back, leaned my torso into hers so that I had to stand on my tiptoes, so that I had to clench my stomach to keep my balance, my body rigid beneath her hands. My mother was shorter than me and I could feel her nose against my neck, the puffs of air it was expelling. She loosened her arms, stepped back. "Honey, maybe after you've had that nap, you might consider taking a shower."

I woke up hours later, hungover. It was eight o'clock, dark, the sun already down. There was a tall glass full of a cloudy liquid, pale orange, on my bedside table. A braver woman, a more passionate, a more foolish woman, a woman more honest with herself, more in touch with her feelings—anyway a *different* woman would have opened a window and poured the damn drink out. But I am the woman I am. I am practical and I do not like waste, and I was thirsty. I drank it.

Fresno, 2014

T he game," I said, sip of wine, grimace, "is, one: we go around in a circle; two: we tell each other when it happened."

This was the situation: the babies were down and the moms were drinking. It was me and Sandra and Dominique and Fran, single girls, hair unwashed, breasts leaking. Not Fran's. Fran's kid never figured out the latch and her milk dried up, breasts shriveled. Well, shriveled. Fran weighed ninety pounds at nine months, not an ounce more, hips so narrow you wondered how she got a tampon in never mind a child out. (C-section.) Even hard and full and heavy her breasts had never been bigger than satsumas. Smoother skin, probably. Not that I'd seen them, Fran's breasts, but you'd think, you'd have to hope. She was a washed-out blonde, hair and skin the same lemon-yogurt color.

Dominique and Sandra and I were legal secretaries at the same firm. A big firm but still, some kind of coincidence. Eight months between Dominique's daughter and my son, Sandra's daughter in the middle, and not a father in sight. Sandra and Fran lived in the same apartment building, a water-damaged dump northeast of downtown, a few streets up from Shaw. They'd met in the laundry room. Fran had been folding a onesie. I recognized her, Fran said. Not from around the building, I mean I saw her and I knew she was a mom. Just *knew*. I rolled my eyes. We didn't call ourselves a book club.

I wasn't drunk but I was drunker than they were. When I suggested the game, I mean. The conversation. Eight months of pregnant sobriety and another twelve breast-feeding and not trusting myself to pump and dump and now one glass of wine was enough to get me tipsy. Two and I'd be spilling secrets, trying and failing to wink. Not that I didn't trust myself to pump and dump properly. More that I didn't trust my body, suspected it might keep some alcohol in reserve, hide the ethanol in my ducts, release it when next my son fed. It seemed like something a new mom shouldn't be allowed to get away with, drinking with her friends while her baby slept. *Louche* was the word that came to mind. Also *lazy* also *bad*. I wasn't raised Catholic but I had somewhere acquired the sensibility. Anyway I imagined it was wrong and that my body would therefore find a way to ensure I didn't get away with it.

But I'd recently weaned my son and one of the moms, Dominique probably, offered me a glass of wine and why not. Dominique was French and so carried with her a particular air of authority. In her presence excess was authorized, encouraged. She'd eaten raw fish and soft cheeses all nine months, drunk red wine, and look at Élise, she was fine, perfectly fine. That air of authority: it also prevented me from asking how a French girl had ended up in the ugliest part of California farm country.

Yes, it must have been Dominique who poured me that first drink, Dominique not taking *no* for an answer, telling me it would loosen my shoulders, help me sleep, and then I was halfway through my second glass of sour white and I was clearing my throat and saying, "What if we played a game." Dominique looked at me, one eyebrow raised, and it occurred to me that her encouraging me to drink, in part it was a perverse curiosity. And why not, sip of wine, grimace, let her have her fun. Fun here was hard to come by if your hopes soared higher than the second story of an air-conditioned shopping complex. We single mothers more or less had to make our own.

"When what happened?" This was Sandra. Sandra was slightly older than the rest of us. Not that the rest of us were young, mid-thirties, late thirties, but Sandra was in her early forties, married twice and divorced twice, thought she was too old to get pregnant, got sloppy with birth control. Or so I imagined. It was in her apartment that we gathered, and sometimes, though not on this occasion, she furnished snacks, thin, greasy blondies, crackers and sweaty chunks of mild cheddar cheese. Effort marked her difference as much as age. Not that the rest of us had given up, just that you could see her trying. *Or so I assumed* because we did not, though some of us had known each other for years, though we had been gathering in Sandra's apartment for months now, putting our babies down in her spare bedroom, the babies arranged in a circle around Sandra's single baby monitor, despite all this, we did not, did not *ever,* discuss our lives *before*. Not who the father was, not our relationship with him. Not our mothers and their eagerness to spoil the baby versus their desire to judge us. Not siblings or first loves or difficulties dating or which members of our families did and did not help with babysitting. Dominique and Sandra had been at the firm when I was hired and I didn't know where they'd worked before. I didn't know where Fran worked, period. Sandra's two marriages, her two divorces, I was just inventing. Anyway, I was tipsy and it seemed suddenly not just odd to me but wrong, this not-knowing.

"I mean," I said, "how we got here. Not the baby part, not how we got pregnant, who the guy was. I mean, you can tell that, too. But what I mean is the moment when getting here, to this room"—I gestured with both hands, pointing down at Sandra's thin carpet as if it might be possible to misunderstand which room I meant—"with the wine and the kid and the no partner, the moment when that became inevitable." Sandra's carpet was a collection of stiff loops, the loops the color of brown rice.

Fran coughed. I suspected her of having some kind of benefactor. Not because she lived well but because on her own I could not imagine her living at all. Not just her breasts seemed shriveled, her face, too, her nose a hard beak and the skin behind it sloping away. Sometimes I saw Fran holding her son, improbably large, his legs a procession of plump rolls, the tendons in her upper arms visible as she lifted him above her head, her son giggling and Fran making a noise with her mouth, the noise trying to sound like the word *whee* but coming out labored, coming out scratchy and choked, and I wondered that she didn't drop him. My son, a shriveled raisin in comparison, like a snack for Fran's or maybe like the wrinkled shit he'd taken after eating his pureed peas. And breast milk was supposed to be so good for a kid. When she cradled her son, stroked his forehead with her long fingers, it was easier to understand, Fran's strength. A witch in a fairy tale, hunched over her prize.

"Look," I said, swallowing the rest of my wine, putting the glass down on the coffee table, "I'll start. I'll start so you can see what I mean.

"How I got here is I started dating a guy at work," I said. "Jeff. His name was Jeff." This was not true. "I was twenty, still in college, this was the summer between junior and senior year, so technically this wasn't a job, it wasn't *work*, it was an internship." This was mostly true. I didn't intend to make my story all the way up, but I did want, for no important reason, for my story to be unverifiable, for Jeff to be untraceable. "He was older, married. Not so much older, early forties, and I was twenty, an adult." Dominique had settled into her chair, stuffed, its fabric patterned, busy. Her father was French and she'd been raised in Avignon but her mother was South African, had emigrated in her twenties, and so Dominique's accent in English was not purely French, had in it also something adjacent to British. Her eyes were closed, and her lips were curved in a smile. We'd had lunch a few times, Dominique and I; dinner once and, over dinner, conversation. She'd cooked for me in her apartment, small but well-appointed, leather and blond wood and thick, spotless velvet, and in a neighborhood in the city's northeastern-most corner, a neighborhood in which I could not afford to live. I'd noticed her bookshelves, built-in, custom-made she told me, noticed they were filled with books. The first functional bookshelves I'd seen since I'd moved from Los Angeles. It was important to me that Dominique find my story interesting. "Two kids," I continued, "a boy and a girl. I looked the girl up recently. She's in her freshman year at Penn. Blond hair, straight teeth, plays field hockey. No visible damage." Not Penn, a less prestigious school. Otherwise accurate. Well, to the best of my knowledge. "Anyway." I shrugged. "It didn't work out. Obviously. The summer ended, I went back to school. I say *back* but the internship was in New York and school was in New York and of course because the internship was in New York Jeff was also in New York and for a while we kept seeing each other. And Jeff told me, kept telling me, that he was going to leave his wife." Another shrug. "And I believed him. Though maybe also I knew he wouldn't because around this time I started riding subways out to the end of the line, subways and also escalators, riding them up and down and then up again. I liked being in motion." I was sitting on the floor and now I began picking at Sandra's brown-rice carpet with my thumb and index finger. The escalators were not really meant to be part of the story. "There was one escalator in a shopping complex in Pelham Bay Park I rode a lot. Sort of a two-for-one deal since Pelham Bay Park is the last stop on the uptown 6." My cheeks were hot. I stared at the pale wooden legs of the coffee table. This wood hasn't been stained, I thought. What's the word for that. On the couch I heard Sandra shifting. "You know," I said, "the illusion of movement." Was the word *nude*? *Nude* wood?

Sandra got up and went to the kitchen for more wine. "How long?" asked Dominique. "How long did it last?" In the kitchen, a cabinet being closed. Fran was perched on one arm of the couch. Out of the corner of my eye I could see her thumbing at her phone.

"Nine months. Nine months and I never saw the inside of his apartment. His wife lived there, too, of course, so did the kids, so it was hotels, mostly. He paid. I was in college, he paid for everything, the hotels, dinner out, dresses, a necklace once. He had money, real estate. Real estate law, that's what he specialized in." In fact he'd been a professor. In fact I'd been his research assistant. It made the hotel rooms more impressive, actually, the fact that he was paying for them on an academic's salary. "It wasn't," I said, "about the money. And the sex was good but it wasn't about the sex." Taking dictation, my knees on the couch, a legal pad propped against the pillows, him behind me, my careful cursive, lifting the pen when he moved against me so the ink wouldn't smudge. My cheeks were still hot, were burning.

"What was it about?" Fran's voice, tiny and high. I looked up. The screen of her phone was dark but it was still in her hand. Not expressing interest. She wanted me to get to the point.

"The first time," I said, "we didn't have sex. He took me out to dinner, and then after dinner, we went to a hotel. I can't actually remember now"—I made a sound like a laugh—"how he convinced me, how we got there, subway or cab or on foot. I remember the room. Not a room, a suite: living room, sitting room, bedroom, bathroom." Saying this out loud it occurred to me: family money. He must have had family money. "He took me to the bedroom." Sandra was back and pouring us all wine. Dominique was sitting up straight now, her feet flat on Sandra's brown-rice carpet. She'd had a pedicure recently, her toenails glinted mauve. "And once we were in the bedroom he pushed me onto the bed, arranged my body so that it was facedown. Not rough but firm." Firm enough that I knew he wouldn't mind getting rough. Me making my body limp, pliable. "He put one hand on my neck, one hand on the small of my back. He pressed down, once." Like my body was clay and the bed was a mold. "Then he lifted his hands, stepped back." Waiting for me to set. "I was still fully clothed. I could hear his breath, my breath. Otherwise it was silent." I touched my wine glass. I wanted to pick it up, take a sip, but I couldn't be sure my hands wouldn't shake, the wine wouldn't spill. "And then he said, maybe I twitched or something, he said, Don't move. He said, Don't fucking move. He said, I'm watching you. He said, I'm watching you and if you move I'll know so you better not move. And then, for a long time, nothing. Twenty minutes or so. Then he told me to get back up. We went into the living room or the sitting room, whichever room had the TV, and he turned it on and we watched something. I don't remember what." I was breathing again. I picked my glass up, took a sip of wine, set the glass back down on the coffee table, hands steady. "The thing is," I said, "the whole time he was watching me—I didn't have to *do* anything. There were no choices to make. I closed my eyes, and my arms and legs—like I had melted into the bed but also I was floating. It's not that I fell asleep, just"—I gestured with one hand, flung it out—"inside, just, blank. Like I was hovering above consciousness. Or maybe below, I don't know. His hands were enormous, enormous and hairy, and it hurt when he pressed me down. Just for a moment and not a lot but enough. Enough so that I knew—plus he had this voice, low and full and—but so that I knew not to move. And that I felt beneath his hands—remade in the way that pain, anyway—" I shrugged. "The point is I'm always—my mind's always—there's a *churning* inside, you know? And I know it doesn't seem like"—I shrugged again—"but there's a line, and it runs straight from that hotel room to the hotel room where"—I paused—"the comfort I take, in being told what to do. The fact that I instinctively hate kindness. These things were always—but it wasn't until—"

The monitor on the coffee table crackled. It was mine, his already wrinkled face collapsing in on itself, his breath coming in little gasps, his arms wriggling. I stood.

"I'll go, too." It was Dominique, rising from her chair. "Élise is such a light sleeper, she'll be up in a second if she isn't already."

———

Sandra's spare room was dim, the shades drawn against the glow of the sun now beginning to set outside, a night-light plugged into the socket by the door. I picked my son up and he quieted. Élise was in fact awake though not complaining, blinking up at Dominique through thick, dark lashes. For a few moments we were silent, me pacing beneath the window, jiggling my arms up and down, Dominique sitting cross-legged on the ground. She'd taken a bottle from her bag and was nudging the nipple into Élise's mouth.

"Mine," Dominique said, "told me I should feel lucky." She was whispering. Above her voice, the sound of Élise suckling. "He was older than yours, not married. Divorced I think, no kids. But in other ways it was similar. First job out of college, my boss, sex in the office, that sort of thing." Dominique was turned away from me but I saw her shoulders move up and down in a shrug. "He said I should feel lucky. He said no one else would want me. I know I look— now"—Dominique's shoulders moved again—"but I got braces late and my skin was bad and I had glasses and freshman year I gained all this weight, plus it took me ages to figure out what to do with my hair. My senior year of high school I shaved most of it off thinking that would solve the problem, which it did. It also made me look"—I could hear the smile

in her voice—"like an egg with a bit of hair on top."
Élise was done feeding and Dominique put the bottle down. "He asked me if I was a virgin. He said, I
bet you're a virgin. And I wasn't, not technically, but
I might as well have been." Élise's head was resting
on Dominique's shoulder now and Dominique was
standing. She turned to face me. "Was yours ugly?"
My son's eyes were drooping shut.

"Not particularly. I mean, he wasn't handsome,
either. A little pudgy, thinning hair. Standard-issue
middle-aged white guy."

"Mine was hideous," Dominique said. "I mean
truly repulsive. Short and squat and bowlegged.
Pockmarked and bald and he didn't take care of
himself, his teeth were yellow and his breath was terrible and there was always dirt under his fingernails.
Also hairy, fantastically hairy. That's what made me
think of it, the fact that yours had hairy hands." She
smiled. "And he was telling me"—the smile became a
grimace—"later I understood that his ugliness gave
him power. Or anyway it made him mean, and if
you're a man, a white man, being mean, usually you
get what you want." She paused. "But I think also he
could see the ugliness in women, I mean, how ugly
they believed themselves to be. It was some kind
of superpower he had. Because by then I'd lost the
weight, I wasn't breaking out, the braces were off, I'd
figured out contacts—but it was like he could see me

at fifteen and sixteen and seventeen and eighteen. He could see, in my head, he could see that was still what I thought I looked like."

We were both pacing now, jiggling our arms, moving in opposite directions, passing each other under the window.

"Did you believe him?"

"About what?

"About being lucky."

"You know," Dominique said, "I think I did. And more than that, I think I was relieved. To know that someone who found me so unattractive—he was always telling me how badly I dressed, how my breasts were too small, how I needed to lose more weight—still wanted to—" Dominique paused. Élise was asleep again and Dominique settled her into her carrier. She stood up and faced me and cupped her hands around my son's small ears. "Still wanted," she said, "to fuck me." She smiled. "To be fair, my clothes *were* terrible. But I think I thought that made him special. And that that made me lucky. Lucky to have found this guy who was nice enough to overlook all the things that were wrong with me. Which, I mean, now I get it. This ugly guy, fifty years old. Of course he was into my twenty-three-year-old pussy. Back then though—" Dominique shook her head. "I was amazed. I swear I was amazed."

Dominique dropped her hands. My son had fallen asleep. Dominique stepped outside and I closed the door softly behind her, kneeled to settle my son in his car seat.

"Home Depot."

"Home Depot?" Fran looked at Sandra.

"You said"—and now Sandra was looking at me—"you wanted to know how we got here. When it happened. The moment when the wine and the kid and the no partner, when those things became inevitable. Well." Sandra sipped her white wine. "The short answer is I went to Home Depot." Raised eyebrows, raised glasses, eyes moving, and a look that flashed, or was it my imagination, between Dominique and me. "My husband," Sandra continued, "my husband at the time"—another sip of wine—"wanted to build me a desk. It was a present. A thoughtful present." Fran put her phone back in her purse, the gesture indicative of respect if not interest. "I'd been talking for years," Sandra said, "about going back to school. Not full-time. Just taking a few night classes. I wanted to learn how to draft." Rueful smile. The wine glass was on the table now and she twisted its stem. "I knew it was too late to become an architect. You need a graduate degree, and even after the degree, you have to apprentice. It's not called an apprenticeship, not anymore, but that's the word for it. Long hours, total deference. The word *junior* in front of your title. And I was already forty, forty-one, I wasn't going to spend three years working fifty-hour weeks for a man a decade younger. Not if my business cards also read *junior*." Another sip of wine. "Not that I would necessarily have had business cards. Anyway"—clearing-away hand motion—"I'm stalling. Sorry." She smiled. "Sorry, I'm nervous. I'm not used to talking about—" She shook her head, cleared her throat. "Anyway. I wanted to learn how to draft. But to draft you need tools, protractor, ruler, sharp pencils, you need, obviously, you need skills, and on top of all that you need also a large horizontal surface. I could buy the tools. I could learn the skills. And my husband said he would take care of the surface. He said he would build me a desk." She was twisting the stem of the glass again, stalling again. "He was a kind man. Is a kind man. Kind and thoughtful and he wanted to make me happy. That's why he sent me to Home Depot. He wanted me to pick out the wood and the stain. He offered to go with me, but I said I would go alone. It felt more"—she shrugged— "like a surprise that way. I imagined folding up the piece of paper on which I'd written my desires and giving this piece of paper to my husband. I imagined forgetting what it was I'd written down. I imagined, some months later, getting exactly what I wanted, how it might, if I were lucky, feel like accident, like serendipity, rather than design. Rather than my design, I mean. How it might feel like *his* design." More shrugging. "He was good at giving gifts. Is good. I mean, I imagine. We've stopped exchanging

gifts for"—hand motion—"obvious reasons." Sandra's lips looked like they had wrapped themselves
around an especially sour slice of lemon. I think she
was trying to smile. "Can I," she said, "get anyone
more wine?" "Please," I said. I did not need more
wine but I sensed Sandra's anxiety, remembered her
trip to the kitchen during my story, forgave her the
insult, hastily drained my glass, warmth flooding my
body, the warmth partly self-satisfaction. "I'd love
some more white." Sandra rose and went to fetch
another bottle and I looked at Dominique and yes,
there was, in her eyes, a kind of interest, a spark of
complicity. Awareness of what I had done for Sandra and gratitude and sympathy. I was tipsy, yes, but
also I was grace itself. There is, below the surface of
every conversation in which intimacies are shared,
an erotic current. Sometimes this current is so hot
it all but boils and other times it's barely lukewarm,
hardly noticeable, but always the current is present,
if only you plunge your hands just an inch or two
farther down in the water. This is regardless of the
gender of the people involved, of their sexual orien-
tations. This is the natural outcome of disclosure,
for to disclose is to reveal, to bring out into the open
what was previously hidden. And that unwrapping,
that denuding, is always, inevitably sensual. Nothing binds two people like sharing a secret. One of
the secrets I imagined Dominique and I sharing: our
dislike of Fran. Call it hatred. Outsized emotions are

easiest to summon when the stakes are low. When Sandra returned, Dominique and I both accepted more wine. Fran shook her head. I thought the word *uncharitable*. Though it also made sense: she'd barely touched her wine, which, fair, she was small enough a thimble would do for a shot glass.

"By the time," Sandra said, her voice lower now, she was speaking more slowly, "I went to that Home Depot, we'd been married almost twenty years. And we'd been trying for a child for almost ten. By trying I mean, just, you know"—a hurry-up motion with her right hand—"nothing fancy, just not being careful. We wanted a kid but we didn't"—she shrugged—"we didn't want to push it. I'd had, in that decade—" She inhaled, said this next part quickly, "Two miscarriages and an ectopic pregnancy," exhaled. "So by the time, well—we figured it wasn't going to happen and we'd made our peace. Russ, that was my husband, Russ had younger sisters and they had kids and I was a beloved aunt, am still a beloved aunt. Well." She smiled. "Perhaps slightly less beloved. Anyway. I was going to learn how to draft and Russ was getting into woodworking, obviously, he was building me the desk, I mean, we'd figured it out. We weren't unhappy." Sandra sighed. "But then I went to this Home Depot. I picked out the wood and I picked out the stain and I wrote the names down on a piece of paper and I picked up a level, which Russ had asked me to buy since I was going to Home

Depot anyway, and I got in line. And in line, in front of me, there's this couple. A boy and a girl. I close my eyes and I can still see the backs of their heads at the moment I become aware of them. Two normal heads with normal hair, totally unremarkable. Kids, both of them. Well, kids to me, in fact they were probably in their early twenties. She has her arm around his waist and her head on his shoulder and she's leaning into him like she's trying to get every part of her body as close to every part of his body as she can. This kind of physical intimacy, that's how I can tell they're young. I mean, there's the clothes and the pimples on his chin that he keeps poking at with his finger, and how smooth her skin is, but the thing I notice first is how she's leaning into him, and only kids do that in public, little kids with their parents, wrapping their bodies around mommy's leg, and big kids with their boyfriends and their girlfriends. Like if they're together, doesn't matter where, they're not going to waste that time, that precious time, being even inches apart. It's a little—I mean it's a *lot*, sometimes, to look at, that kind of need, in public. It can be—well, it can be disgusting. Especially if they're also kissing and usually they are. But there's something, or, looking at these kids I felt also there was something, *sacred* isn't the word, but they were treating this mundane moment, Sunday afternoon in a crowded Home Depot, waiting in line to check out, they were respecting this moment, they were insisting it was too good and special a moment not to honor with this display. There was a kind of, I don't know, reverence to it. Gross as it also was. A kind of honesty."

Sandra sighed. "I'm stalling again. But okay what happens next is basically nothing. What happens next is the girl, she has this really long, sort of light brown hair, not mousy, what I guess you'd call honey-colored, and not straight, it's got a little wave, a little muss to it—I mean, it was a little greasy, too, if I'm being completely honest—and he turns his body toward hers and he lifts her hair, he takes this big handful of hair and he lifts it off her neck, and she's got this—she's got this extraordinary, this neck, this long, thin, pale neck. And I mean nothing about this couple is elegant, she's wearing sweatpants and he's wearing basketball shorts, and so this neck—it's sort of shocking, this neck belongs on a ballerina, not on some— Anyway, out comes this beautiful neck and he leans down and kisses her, tenderly, this soft little peck, right behind her ear, where the neck starts to turn into head. And, like, okay, this is definitely gross. Like, my usual attitude toward this kind of display is *Get a room*, is, *Some of us are just trying to buy levels here*. But what I feel, looking at them, it's not frustration or annoyance or disgust. What I feel is something"—she clenched one hand—"in my chest tightening, something in my stomach falling, and—and this is the part that, in that moment, I am completely confounded by, because what I also feel is—" A pause. "What I'm confused by is that these feelings, they're coming from—" Another pause. "I'm older and maybe there's not a ton of romance in my life and you'd expect, I mean *I* would expect to feel a kind of envy of the girl, of her youth and the intensity of her desire and the intensity of this guy's desire for her. But what I feel"—intake of breath— "what I want, actually, is to be the one kissing her neck. It's like when, when you go to the eye doctor and they're checking your prescription, when they're getting close to the right one and they slide the, whatever it is, the glass with the right magnification in front of your eye and suddenly the blurry chart on the wall that you've been looking at sort of jumps into focus. All my life, witnessing these scenes, I'd been imagining myself as the girl and feeling, you know"—Sandra shrugged—"feeling like *This is the thing I'm supposed to want,* feeling like *Okay, sure, seems like I want it,* and all of a sudden there's like this"— she snapped her fingers—"the right glass slides down and there's this jump and I realize, Oh no, it's the *guy,* I want to be the *guy.*" Sandra sighed, shook her head, took another sip of wine. "I think I stole the level," Sandra said. "I know I stepped out of the line, I remember bumping, sort of crashing, into whoever it was behind me, I was in such a hurry. I know I left the store. And now Russ owns a level, so. But so I get home and there's my husband and he's sitting in the living room of the house we own and he's eating off of one of the plates his mother gave us as a wedding present and it seems so clear, it seems so clear that this is my life. And the moment at the Home Depot, it gets"—Sandra waved a hand—"put away. I mean, later of course I think back over my"—she grimaced—"sexual history, how uninterested I was in dating all throughout high school and college, how I married the first man I slept with, how the best thing I can say about my sex with him is that it is never unpleasant, and certain things become— But women aren't supposed to enjoy sex, right? I mean, this is what I was raised, what I've been telling— Anyway." Sandra laughed, a sharp bark of a laugh. "Three days later I miss my period. Which is actually comforting because it helps explain what happened at the Home Depot, right? My hormones were all over the place, signals got crossed, thank god I didn't, you know, bring it up with Russ. The next few weeks are just waiting. Waiting in doctors' offices, waiting by the phone for test results. Russ and I decide that if the amniocentesis doesn't come back clean we'll abort. We remind ourselves there's a chance the procedure itself will cause a miscarriage. Basically we're trying not to get our hopes up. And we're not telling anyone so that in case it doesn't work out, which it probably won't, we won't have to—" Sandra swallowed the last of her wine, poured herself another glass. "Anyway, we're trying to prepare ourselves. But then we make it ten weeks, twelve weeks, fourteen. I get the amnio and I don't miscarry and it comes back clean and we're at sixteen weeks, eighteen, twenty, twenty-two, twenty-four. We call our parents, we tell our friends. And now it's real, it's happening, this thing we've wanted for so long. I'm pregnant. I'm going to have a child.

"And maybe this isn't unexpected or unusual, but I should say," Sandra continued, "that my pregnancy was a nightmare. Morning sickness all day for the first three months, couldn't keep anything but saltines and Gatorade down. I started keeping—this is embarrassing but," Sandra laughed, the sound lower and gentler, "no more embarrassing than anything else I've shared so far. I started keeping an empty trash can by my desk just in case I couldn't make it to the bathroom. Made sure there was always a fresh trash bag in it. I only used it a couple times but that was enough, my whole cube reeked of bile for weeks. Though that could have been my imagination, I was so sensitive to smells then, if someone walked by eating a banana I'd feel nauseous for hours. And my teeth hurt. And then my hair started falling out and my nails stopped growing and somehow I was losing weight. This was in the first two, three months. Real horror-movie stuff. But so then at sixteen weeks, this is right after the amnio, I start gaining weight. A lot of weight. Fifteen, twenty pounds, like, overnight. And I *keep* gaining weight, more than I'm supposed to be gaining, the line on the chart is, like, exponential. And suddenly nothing fits, not even my maternity stuff, and my ankles start swelling and I'm hungry all the time, starving. I buy these enormous overalls and I start living in them when I'm not at the office. For the office I have a series of shapeless cotton dresses, these sort of really depressing curtains—I mean, you must have seen me wearing them. And Crocs. I'd squeeze my feet into flats when I had to go into meetings, but in my cube I wore compression socks under Crocs, that's pretty much all that fit.

"Anyway." Sandra exhaled, set her glass, half empty, down on the table. "I'm five months pregnant. I'm so hungry after work that I'm buying an entire rotisserie chicken on my way home at least twice a week, parking my car in the driveway and picking the carcass clean, throwing the bones in the trash before I walk into the house. I'm waking up in the middle of the night and driving to diners for fried pickles and a milkshake. I'm putting ranch dressing on everything, going through a bottle or two a week. People start asking me if I'm having twins. Start telling me I look ready to pop. Saying things like *You know, my kid was a couple weeks overdue, too, it's not a big deal, sometimes they just need a little extra time to bake.* And as soon as they say *bake* I'm thinking, Hey, it's been twenty minutes since I last ate, I'm *hungry.*

"So I'm at five months, five and a half. This is a Saturday afternoon. I'm driving home from the movie theater. I've started going to the movies once, twice a week. Or, actually, what I've started doing is buying movie tickets so I can get inside the movie theater so I can get to the snacks. The nacho cheese dip they serve, I'm addicted to it. Can't find it anywhere else. And sure, I could tell the ticket taker, Look, I'm pregnant, I need some nacho cheese, I'm not going to see a movie, can you just let me in. But somehow that's more embarrassing than buying a ticket for"—Sandra waved a hand—"one of the *Hunger Games* movies. Now I can't even remember which one, and I must have bought tickets to it ten or twelve times, going theater to theater, just in case someone got suspicious. I mean suspicious of— Anyway. This one day, it's a Saturday, a Saturday afternoon, I'm driving back from the movie theater, one hand on the wheel, one hand in the nacho cheese sauce, and one minute I'm driving by a strip mall with a Home Depot in it, with *the* Home Depot in it, and the next I'm parking my car.

"And even now I don't—I mean, what did I think would happen? That the same couple would be there again? And even—I mean even if, by some wild coincidence, they *had* been, there wasn't anything— Maybe I would have followed them around the store? And if I had, honestly, I don't—I don't know what I was hoping for. Some kind of magic, obviously, but whether I wanted the—the moment, the feeling, I'd experienced before, whether I wanted it replicated or explained or whether I wanted it somehow reversed, I—" Sandra trailed off. She cleared her throat. "They weren't there. Obviously. Instead I wandered up and down the aisles for a while. Not that long. The pregnancy had given me sciatica and walking for more than fifteen, twenty minutes was painful. I got gestational diabetes in the sixth month. Not exactly a surprise. I'm sorry," Sandra said after a pause, "I guess this story is a little anticlimactic because it more or less ends here. I walked around Home Depot for a while and eventually my back started hurting and I left. And walking out I was fine, walking back to the car I was fine, and then in the car I started crying. I started crying and I couldn't stop. I was still crying when I got home. Russ told me it was just pregnancy hormones. That's what he said when I came home sobbing and said I needed to move out. That wasn't—" Sandra was speaking slightly slower now. "I don't want to make him seem— that wasn't the first thing he said. He wasn't cold. Wasn't unsympathetic. The opposite, actually. First thing, he got me a box of tissues. Made me a cup of chamomile tea. We sat down on the couch together and he wrapped me in a blanket"—she touched the blanket behind her—"this blanket, actually, and he rubbed my swollen feet and I tried to explain it to him." Sandra smiled. "Which was hard. Because I didn't know what I was trying to explain to him. I just knew that I'd—that I'd seen something. And

that I'd tried to—to put it away. And that I couldn't.
And if I couldn't, it wasn't honest. Being married to
him. It just wasn't fair." Sandra drank until her glass
was empty and then she set the glass down. She did
not refill it. "I don't"—she paused—"I don't believe
in moments, really. Everything takes time. Me moving out, that took time, and working out a custody
agreement, that took forever. And I'm still in the
middle of figuring—but you said," Sandra sighed,
"you said *moment*. So. Okay. That moment in the
Home Depot. If I had to pick one." Sandra's cheeks
were flushed pink and there was a sheen of sweat on
her forehead. "Does anyone," she said, standing, fan-
ning herself with one hand, the now-empty bottle
of white she'd brought in from the kitchen in the
other, "want any more wine?"

I snuck a sleeve of saltines from Sandra's kitchen
and went into the bathroom to eat them, but then
it turned out I also had to pee, which meant resting
the sleeve on the edge of the sink while I pulled my
jeans down, maternity jeans with the stretchy side
panels, the only pair that fit, and underneath them
the high-waist control-top bottoms I still reinforced
with panty liners because giving birth vaginally had
weakened the muscles of my pelvic floor and that
made bladder control more challenging, or so my gynecologist said. Practically it meant I could no longer
consistently *hold it*. Only I had already opened the

sleeve of saltines, before resting them on the ledge of the sink I mean, so that when, peeing, I reached over to grab them, I discovered that the first five or six saltines were now damp and several more had probably come into contact with the ledge though they retained no physical evidence of this encounter, which meant that they, too, would have to be dumped. I stopped peeing, dropped ten or so saltines into the bowl, resumed peeing, began snacking. There was a logic to it. I mean, I didn't want to eat the saltines with presumably soiled hands, post-pee, and to wash with both hands would require setting the saltines down again, and them possibly getting wet again, and then having to dump more, and I needed to eat all of the remaining saltines, plus to gulp some water directly from the faucet, if I was going to drive home. Peeing, eating, I wondered how profoundly I had embarrassed myself. Not telling my story, no, Sandra's story had been just as shaming, its telling neutralizing, retroactively justifying, mine. No it was the connection I'd imagined with Dominique that I was pondering, peeing, how I'd tilted my body toward her as I leaned over my wine glass, hoping she'd look down, see the shape of my breasts, my shirt was a V-neck and some of the pregnancy weight had settled, as weight I gain always does, in my tits, which were now, still, though I was no longer breast-feeding, surprisingly full above the cage of my ribs. I'd hoped then that she'd notice them, my tits, and I hoped now, peeing, that she hadn't, that she hadn't noticed me trying to get her to notice. To flirt was to expose one's desires, an act inherently shaming. Not that I'd been flirting, exactly, my attraction to Dominique was not sexual, just as my attraction to Artemisia had not been sexual, not exactly, though in both cases the attraction was also hungry, was also greedy. It wasn't that I wanted to fuck Dominique it was that I wanted to devour her. Wanted her to devour me. At this time I imagined intimacy as a kind of literal entanglement, which perhaps explains why, when the thrill of an intimacy newly forged wore off, my first and most powerful desire was to run. In my defense it's very hard to get much of anything done if you're physically attached to a second person.

I finished peeing and finished the saltines and wiped and flushed and washed my hands and gulped some water. To indicate interest is already to expose oneself to humiliation. To admit the existence of a desired object is to admit that to be rejected by the desired object, to admit that the desired object's disappearance, one of the two always inevitable, even if only in death, will be painful. Or maybe it's that to desire something is to believe that you know it, and if you're wrong about the knowing you feel foolish and if you're right you're still wrong because to know something or someone in one moment is to know a version of that thing or person that can only exist temporarily, that must and will eventually change, that cannot and will not ever reassume the precise form in which you first desired it. Anyway, probably Dominique had taken my interest as a simple interest in friendship, which it also was and which was also embarrassing, to desire this different and lesser kind of intimacy, but less so, not as embarrassing as wanting to devour her, not so embarrassing that it would be impossible to face her at work, at our next gathering, should I run into her at the grocery store, etc. In short, *could have been worse* was my ultimate determination as I dried my hands. Having reached this conclusion I allowed myself to indulge the thought that I had been nursing since the end of Sandra's story, which was that only someone born and raised in this ass-end, middle-of-nowhere, this so-mediocre-only-clichés-can-describe-its-mediocrity, this alleged *city* whose culture was as dead as the land surrounding it was fertile, only someone born and raised here could, one, have a lesbian conversion at the age of are you *kidding* me forty-one in, two, a Home Depot, and, three, manage not *only* to experience homosexual desire along the vector of heterosexual desire but *also,* in her interpretation of that homosexual, that is quote-unquote *nontraditional,* desire, reify *traditional* gender roles in the most stereotypical way. I tossed the saltine sleeve in the bowl and flushed again. *You,* I said to my reflection in the mirror, *are a real bitch.* Perhaps, I thought as I left the bathroom, I could sneak one more sleeve of saltines from Sandra's kitchen on the way back to the living room, stash them in my purse, eat them in my parked car before I drove home, which was not, thankfully, so far away.

In the living room, Sandra was collecting glasses and Dominique was standing, rummaging in her purse. Fran was looking at her phone. I stashed the crackers in my own purse, was heading to the spare bedroom to collect my son, when I heard Fran's voice, high, thin, already, *always already,* pitched at a whine. "Wait," she said, "don't you want to hear my story?" Sandra was bent over the coffee table, reaching for a wine glass. Fran's head swiveled from right to left. "The kids aren't even up yet." This was true. Though also Dominique had not told a story, not to the group at least, which meant that no one wanting to hear Fran's story—and I took for granted that no one did—could be chalked up to accident rather than malice. Two out of the four of us had bared our souls, the wine was gone, it was getting late, we should be getting home now, shouldn't we, the babies would want their own beds.

Sandra stood. She set the wine glass back down. "Fran," she said, "I think everyone wants to—"

"No," Fran said. She didn't raise her voice. She didn't stand, sound angry, just the whine, which was always there, growing, yes, I'm afraid the word is *shrill*. "No," she said again. "No, you need to lis-

ten to what I have to say." Sandra sat back down.
I slid two saltines into my mouth. Dominique sat,
her phone in her hand. She glanced down, typing,
maybe she was sending a text. "Look, you're all imagining yourselves," Fran said, "as people in some kind
of *story*." The way she said *story*, like it was a dirty
word. "Like you"—she looked at Sandra—"you had a
weird *feeling* in a *Home Depot* and so you just *had* to
leave your husband? Or you"—she looked at me—"so
a guy fucks you over once, and, what, you can't ever
have a healthy relationship again?" She shook her
head. "I don't buy it. Everyone makes choices. Do
you know how many women raise children alone?
We're not *special* because we were left. Or because we
left. A bunch of self-centered—" She shook her head.
"And okay, you all probably think I'm an asshole,
whatever"—she waved her hand—"I don't care. And
I'm not trying to be an asshole, I'm sure you think I
am but I'm not. I could *give* a fuck. The point is, who
cares about understanding *why*. The point is there
is no *reason*. No one has a plan for you and your
life doesn't have a soundtrack, it's just a series of"—
she shrugged—"accidents and split-second decisions
and coincidences and demographics, where you
live and when you were born and who your parents
were and how much money they had." She glared at
me. "I *know* you think I'm an idiot but I'm actually
not. I wanted a supportive group of single mothers
I could share colic stories with, not a bunch of self-

aggrandizing pity partyers. Like anyone *cares*." She shouldered her diaper bag. "And look, for the record, I'm"—she turned to Sandra—"an *actual* lesbian, and how my child was conceived, it's a *fascinating* story. Which I will never tell any of you."

At least this is what I think she said. What I remember her saying. I think at least I got the tone right, her anger, and also the register, the word *demographics* shooting out from between her withered lips, I mean that was memorable. I do tend to think I'm the smartest person in every room and it doesn't help that lately I have been. Fran was, certainly, the first to leave and she did not attend our gatherings after, which were, perhaps understandably, less regular. In the moments after she spoke I remember thinking that if she was in some way correct she was, however, not *right*. That of course life is random, a series of coincidences, etc., but that to live you must attempt to make sense of it, and that's what narrative's for. I believe this, people of a certain sensibility believe this. Mostly it's harmless. Though perhaps sometimes you find yourself doing things because you think the narrative arc calls for it, or because you've grown bored with your own plot, things you shouldn't do because they will, these things, hurt the other characters in your story, who are not characters after all, but people. But then people do evil often and with less elaborate justifications.

Dominique and I collected our children, walked out to our cars together. I'd sobered up, Fran's speech like a slap to the face, my cheeks were even red, though that was probably from embarrassment and/or the wine I'd been drinking. "Well," Dominique said as we reached her car, which was parked a block closer to Sandra's house than mine. "I'll see you tomorrow." I nodded, kept walking, but then Dominique said, "Wait," and I turned around. "Do you think," she said, "what Fran said, about how one guy—" She paused. "I mean, is that what you think happened?" I considered this. "No," I said. "I think, actually"—my back was against Dominique's car now, so that I was facing not her but the other side of the street—"what was deadly about that, that guy, is how much I liked it. Not that he screwed me over but how, later, what I remembered was that it felt—right. I mean I felt, sure, I felt embarrassed, too, describing it, it was so clear how sort of manipulative—but not having to make any decisions. Like, I couldn't call him, he could only call me. And since he had a family, since he had all these family commitments, if I wanted to see him it had to be when he had time, even if I was busy. It felt—I mean it also felt terrible, I never knew, I could never quite trust—and if I ever got upset because I wanted to see him more, because I wanted to introduce him to my friends he'd get cold, just immediately he'd shut down, he'd never try to comfort me or apologize or—he'd just shut down, usually he'd just leave and if I was lucky after a few hours he'd come back and I'd better be done crying. But when I thought about it, especially right after, right after it ended, usually what I remembered was feeling like—like *oh*, this is what I can do, this is what I'm meant to be used for. I do know"— I looked over at Dominique—"I do know how that sounds. But basically the problem was I liked not having to decide. And so that meant, one, this kept happening to me, this kind of guy, and, two, when I did try to decide, I mean romantically, I just— I was just no good at it. Both because I didn't have any practice and because I couldn't trust myself, couldn't trust my gut when it told me what I wanted because apparently what I wanted was a married guy whose house I wasn't allowed to see." I smiled at Dominique. She did not smile back. "Um," I said, "what about you? What"—I shifted the weight of my son's car seat from my right arm to my left—"what do you think happened? To you?" "Well," she said, "for a bit after, I hated myself. At first because of course eventually he stopped sleeping with me and then later because I realized what he had been, what I had let—what I *felt* like I had let happen. And then I didn't trust anyone, and then I was angry. I slept with a lot of men during the angry bit, I was rather cruel to them. And then," Dominique said, and she raised her eyebrows, "I went to therapy and sorted a lot of this out. Have you considered therapy?" "Oh god," I said, laughing, "on my salary? On our health plan?" "I could give you some names," Dominique said, "if you wanted. A lot of therapists, good ones, work on a sliding scale." I shifted the car seat again and smiled, shook my head. I had imagined us as allied, allied in our difference: her with the accent and the functional bookshelves, me with my *all but* PhD. Okay by *difference* I mean *superiority*. "That's so nice of you." I was walking backward, toward my car. But if she thought the answer was *therapy*, well. "Let me think about it?" Dominique shrugged, opened the passenger-side back door. "Offer's on the table," she said.

I know how this sounds; I mean, *now* I know how it sounds. Then I thought *Excuse me this is a* very *interesting story I'm telling you about* me, *a* very *interesting person,* I thought *If you think I need* therapy *because of it the word for* that *is* pathologizing, I thought *And* also *I never liked you that much anyway.* "Right," I said, shouting now, "thanks again." I had almost reached my car. "See you tomorrow!"

My son didn't wake up on the way home. Didn't wake up when I stopped at Vons to get a bottle, a couple bottles, of white wine, didn't wake up when I lifted him from the car and carried him into the house, back then he slept well, slept soundly. I settled him into his crib, uncorked one of the bottles, poured myself a glass. As a child I'd watched a television show in which a girl, half-human, half-alien, was able to stop time by pointing her index fingers toward each other and joining them. Her father, the alien, was a cube of some kind? A trapezoidal quartz crystal? I poured myself another glass of wine and tried the thing with the index fingers, knowing nothing would happen, treating the trick as a sobriety test, passing it, congratulating myself. If it were possible to stop time, I thought, I'd take a week, maybe two. Read some books. Develop a meditation *practice*. See a therapist, fine, *sure*. Journal. Get my story straight. The problem wasn't thinking of myself as the protagonist of a narrative it was that I hadn't figured out the right narrative yet. I just needed one that looked less like a bell curve, and me on the downward slope, and more like a tangent, a tangent to a vertical. A vertical line meant x equaled a constant, I remembered that. Yes, me and the kid, my son, zooming up the y, bigger and better things in the future for both of us. I poured myself another glass of wine. Truth didn't help. Everything that had ever happened could never be integrated into something coherent. The trick was picking the right moments. The trick was knowing when to lie. I'd drained my third glass, part of a fourth wouldn't hurt, two-thirds of a glass, three-quarters. I'd stashed bourbon somewhere, the trick was finding it. Drinking now, white wine or maybe bourbon, maybe two glasses in front of me, drinking first from one and then from the other, thinking, What's the story, thinking, What's the story, Morning Glory, was that an album, maybe British, thinking, You are the master of your destiny, thinking I missed the weight of a body on mine, how the weight tamed and taught my body, how easy it was for my body, under a weight, to do nothing but be. Thinking one more drink couldn't hurt. Thinking I wasn't so old now, was I, thinking in the morning I'd get another shot, another shot at getting it right, getting it all right, making it all right, and this was the last thought I had, the last I remember, before falling asleep, my hand on a glass, the baby monitor waking me three hours later, my son's sharp, wordless cries, my head resting on my shoulder, my neck sore from the awkwardness of the position, his cries impossible to interpret, no time to think. All I had to do was respond.

Santa Barbara, 2016

I tell people—" She paused. "When I tell people. If I tell people. I tell them I gave the baby up." We were, she and I, swimming. "People assume I mean adoption. If I don't bother to correct them." Her shoulders rose and then fell. "It's not a lie, not exactly." We'd met earlier that day, our carts colliding at a supermarket. "After all," she said, "I did." Another pause. "I did give the baby up." This woman, I don't remember her name. What I do remember: it was dark. The body of water in which we swam was the Pacific and though the water was cold I was not uncomfortable. The water pressing against my body and my body pressing back, pressing through: the experience was one of minor but continual triumph. Of resistance, again and again, overcome. Yes, my primary feeling was one of pleasure. Sustained pleasure, that is, luxury. I rolled the word *luxury* from the back to the front of my mouth, the underside of my tongue, smooth and slick, sliding against the roof of my mouth. Also we were both naked, both drunk. If this does not explain the situation perhaps it may explain something about the kind of woman who would find herself in it. Often, when I tell this story, as I have been encouraged to in therapy and in group and by my mother, I say that I picked her, this nameless woman, up. Not because it makes more sense, though it does. Because that phrase, *I picked her up,* my listeners find it provocative. Provocative as in *to provoke,* as in *to provoke interest.* I've said it before and I'll say it again: conversation is flirtation. Tease out enough rope and the listener, she'll hang on your every word. Though it's true: usually I am the one left hanging. This woman, for example, she certainly had me on the line. Why is it that people tell me things? I think it is because I like, liked, to drink and I am good at keeping my face quiet. Also because I ask questions. What I had asked her: "Do you have any kids?" This is female socialization, that is, the desire to be everywhere approved of, carried to its logical extreme.

It was a Saturday. Earlier that day I'd left my son with a babysitter, gotten in my car. It was summer. Ten in the morning and the air in the Central Valley was already dry as sandpaper, never mind hot. In the cup holder nearest my ever-outstretched hand, a thermos of coffee. A thermos of coffee and bourbon. Maybe one-third bourbon, two-thirds coffee. Maybe one-third coffee, two-thirds bourbon. These details are hard to remember. Also I may be exaggerating them. Also I may be minimizing them. The difference between the two—for when a memory is retold, its particulars, inevitably, are brightened or muted depending on the arc of the story of which it is a part—a question of, determined by, desire. Am I, just now, more interested in appearing openly louche (look at me lapping at *luxury*) or secretly wounded? How close to the surface is my pain? Or, rather, how close to the surface do I want my pain to appear to be? How enamored am I of the clichés of female pain? Or, rather, of which of these clichés am I enamored? Do I wish to make my distress visible and, therefore, hysterical? Or do I wish to suffer in silence? How often do I clean my home? How many loaves of bread do I bake, on average, every week? Careful: do not blame these hard-to-remember details on my child, as cliché might urge. Many women fear losing, in childbirth, in the daily act of mothering, autonomy, independence, selfhood. But I had never had a self I was much interested in keeping and a child will give direction as well as, better than, a married professor. Though the satisfaction in taking direction from a child is mixed with fear. The fear of *who will this child become,* of *what if he turns out to be,* of *will it be my fault.* The fear of *am I doing this right.* The married professor, on the other hand, he tells you if you're doing it right. Yes, he's quite direct. And if the satisfaction he offers is mixed with shame, well, shame is not without its pleasures, not least the pleasure of knowing you deserve to feel it. Anyway, you're not supposed to take direction from a child. Or you're supposed to know when to take it and when not to, and I was, no surprise, bad at telling cases of the former from cases of the later.

And so: my skin itched after too many hours with him. My son. The son I bounced in my arms as I walked the halls of my house. No, not my arms, plural. My arm, singular. The other arm was needed to lift the glass of bourbon to my mouth. I only felt him slip, I only left him in his crib, howling, while I ran to refill the glass, I only let him cry while I held my head, throbbing, these things, really they only happened once or twice. And so, from time to time it became necessary to schedule a reprieve. Driving: this was the reprieve. A way to keep my mind occupied. To distract it from the topic in which it was most interested and which I—here we imagine the *I* as a whole and the *mind* as a part, as *apart*—most wished to avoid. That part being the self and how it was doing. Whether it was *doing it right.* The self being my self. The avoidance stemming from a fear of self-knowledge, the kind of self-knowledge—*no, you are* not *doing it right*—that provokes not merely guilt but the desire for, the necessity of, reformation. Perhaps this is becoming confusing. Sometimes when I drank from the thermos that was either one-third or two-thirds coffee it became confusing, and sometimes it became clear.

The point is, I drove. I drove and listened to the radio. When it got, even with the windows down, too hot in the car, whose air-conditioning was broken, I parked. I located a supermarket, a pharmacy, a department store, and I parked my car and locked my doors and allowed myself, once inside the market, the pharmacy, the store, to wander the aisles. I would hold plastic bottles of probiotics. I would finger bags of savory snacks. I would walk toward my image in the convex mirrors that hung from the ceiling at the back of the store, watching that image, distorted, enlarge, transfixed, so that I did not notice the woman who was then walking down the aisle toward me, the woman who was now swimming beside me, until my cart collided with hers.

"The truth is," the woman said, "I abandoned my child." I'd had a head start, true, but over the course of the afternoon and then the evening, she had caught up. How much I used to drink, it gives other people permission. And how much they then drink, this gives further permission. To speak what might be called, in a certain kind of book, their quote-unquote truth. To confess. The sitter was expecting me, had been expecting me for hours. From where I was I could not see, back on the shore, the indicative glimmer of an incoming call or text. I could not see the screen of my phone blinking on and off, now bright, now dim, now bright again. Soon the sitter would give up on me and call my parents. Would discover that they, too—it was eleven, perhaps eleven-thirty—were too drunk to drive.

The woman had flipped onto her back, was no longer paddling, was breathing, slowly, in and out, her spine on the surface of the water, the palms of her hands cupping the moonlight. Or this is how I remember it. Certainly she was floating. But that phrase, *cupping the moonlight*—it cannot be anything other than a post facto gilding of—well, no, not a lily. The water was, as I said, cold, and my fingers were logged with it. Numb besides. Also where was my car and when would I again be able to drive it. Remember I was drunk. Remember my veins were full of bourbon, my skin flush with it. And so what I remember of this night is not my teeth chattering or the salt water I had swallowed, how it scraped against my sinuses, the back of my throat, what I remember is the feeling of being held. Being held by the water. How hesitant I am to say it. If I could paddle, I thought, in this water forever. In fact even paddling was largely unnecessary, the ocean's salinity, the reliable rhythm of the waves, buoying me, their suck and swell against the soft of my stomach and the hard knock of my ribs. And from this feeling, what I have called *pleasure*, what I have called *luxury*, but which was in fact closer to relief, come phrases like *cupping the moonlight,* come words like *susurrus* to describe the sound of the wind licking at the lapping waves, comes the coincidence of *licking* and *lapping,* of *comes* and *coincidence.* I'll say this: the feeling, whatever I call it, did share in pleasure's abdication of responsibility.

The woman's feet dipped below the surface of the water and she was upright again, paddling, paddling toward me until her breath was louder than the waves and the wind, louder than my own breath, and she said, she was looking at me, or best I could tell she was looking at me, remember it was dark, remember I was drunk, she said, again, "I abandoned my child." And then, quickly, "Her. My child was a girl." More slowly now: "You know, I read somewhere— and of course it's true, self-evident—that even in times of crisis, times of war, under dictatorships, after a natural disaster, people continue— But wait." She lifted a hand from the water. "To understand how it was, how bad it got, how bad I *made* it, you have to know how good I had it. For example: my house, the one I shared with my husband, it was featured in *Architectural Digest.* When we got married, I got two pages in *Brides.* Me in my dress, the train spread, the veil lowered, surrounded by bridesmaids. My flower girl in the foreground spreading petals. Me holding a cream-colored bouquet. His four-year-old niece, his older brother's daughter, she was our flower girl. Not that that particularly—and I know what you're thinking. We were rich, we were beautiful." And she was beautiful, too beautiful to be in a supermarket at five o'clock on a Saturday afternoon, this was perhaps the reason I attempted conversation after my cart collided with hers, clipped her ankle. Being in the company of an exceptionally beautiful woman, all clean lines and precise movements, when I'm sober it makes me feel huge and grubby and spherical, but when I'm drunk, proximity to beauty, it's like being, myself, chosen. "But there wasn't, beneath that, the darkness, the emptiness." She paused. "It's nice to believe that the rich must be, in exchange for their money, unhappy. And surely some are. But we were not. I was not. I am not a depressive person. I have always had a great capacity for happiness, and when we were dating, during the period of our engagement—You know," the woman said, "it's normal for couples to argue when they're planning a wedding. The sheer number of decisions to be made. Plus money, plus family, plus seating arrangements, and how many bridesmaids and who and what color will their dresses be and—" She stopped. "My point is we didn't. Happiness is boring. I mean to describe. Sometimes to live, too, I suppose. For some. Not for me. I was happy. I was happy enough that I didn't think about my own happiness. No. I enjoyed it." Splashing, the sound local, not the waves against the rocks, against the shore. The woman's arms were extended, her back was curved, the smooth semicircle of her body emerged from and then reentered the water as she turned one, two, three backward somersaults. Then her head came up, she was shaking it. "Water in my ears," she said. "Very briefly, I was a competitive synchronized swimmer." Perhaps if she'd been closer to me, if it hadn't been so dark, I would have been able to see her smile. "That's a lie." A brief pause, an intake of breath. "We decided to get pregnant. I wanted a child. He wanted a child. We decided to get pregnant. It happened almost immediately. The pregnancy was easy. Two weeks of morning sickness. I gained twenty pounds, maybe twenty-five, total. This part," she sighed, "I'm sorry but this part is boring. I'm going to skip ahead. I give birth. Also easy. Four hours of labor, start to finish. No epidural. My perineum doesn't tear. No problems breast-feeding. No problems sleeping. The baby weight comes off. The stretch marks fade. This part is boring, too, but it's important—" She paused. "I need you to understand how easy I had it, with the baby. Like I need you to understand how good I had it, with my husband. What else?" She shook her head. "We're both lawyers, my husband, my ex-husband, and I. Our firms are, again, improbably understanding. I take six months of maternity leave, three paid. When I go back to work, he takes three months. When he goes back to work, the baby, the girl, she's nine months old. We get a nanny. We offer a fair wage and reasonable hours and I do not feel any guilt about hiring her. She comes highly recommended and she doesn't disappoint. I make it home in time for bedtime, not every night, but say four nights out of five. On weekends I cook. Saturday nights, we trade off; one week I'll go out after bedtime, catch up with a friend, have a glass of wine, the next it's his turn. It helped that we had money, of course, but we were, also, I can say this now, ten years later, with a certain amount of objectivity, good parents. Together, I mean. A handful of fights—or, not fights. Disagreements. Disagreements we go to couples therapy to work out. And it's going so well it takes me a whole two years to realize—" She laughed. Then a silence. I opened my eyes. Not that I'd been falling asleep, just that total darkness, it heightened the feeling of being not a body but a collection of sensations tied ever so loosely to a brain. "I need you to ask me," she said. "I can't quite"—she smiled— *give myself permission* to say it if you don't ask me. Therapy-speak, sorry." A pause. "Ask me," she said, "what I realized." "What," I said, "did you realize?" Another pause. And then, quickly: "I realized I didn't love my child. My daughter. She has a name but I'm not going to say it. *Jesus* I sound dramatic." She swam a few lengths away from me and then back. "I had never—this seems, now, ridiculous, but it's true—I had never asked myself if I wanted a baby. Children. I was—I am—what I think the kids would call a," she giggled, "a *basic bitch*. I was a real *cunt*. You know I am a real *advocate*, I consider myself a real *champion* of"—she giggled again—"yes a real *champion* of the renaissance of, of the *resuscitation*, of the *reclamation* of the word *cunt*. Like, okay, we can say *asshole*, we can say *dick*, but oh *god*, oh *no*, don't you *dare* try to make a *swear* word out of the *female*—" She broke off. Even drunk the giggles disturbed me. Perhaps, even drunk, they disturbed her, too, because again she paused. "I'm not trying—no, I *am* trying to make light of this. Because I think there's no other way of talking about—" Another pause. "I didn't think about having children because I had myself been a child. It's as simple—as stupid—as that. A woman had given birth to me. I was a woman. I would give birth to someone else. But then the baby came and though everything was—perfect, so much better than almost anyone in this country, in any country, can expect, I didn't"—another pause—"I didn't love her. My baby. My daughter. I felt, toward her—" She swam away again and swam back. My eyes were open now, trained on the edges of her body, what outline the low light illuminated. "I felt nothing. No hate. No resentment. Just—nothing. Toward"—here she swam a bit closer—"toward myself, too. As a mother I did not—recognize myself. Toward myself as a mother I had no feeling." She flipped herself onto her back and I paddled closer so that my head was near hers, so that I could be sure of hearing what she said next. "It may have been postpartum depression. But the hardest part of this to admit, the part that feels the most shameful, the reason I don't tell anyone—it's the fact that I don't feel guilty. I don't regret it. The decision I made. I feel certain it was the right one." She turned herself so that she was upright in the water again. "I was saying, earlier. About how during bad times, well—life goes on. It's a cliché but it's a cliché because it is, on some level, on the deepest level, true. It's something I find frustrating about— you know those big historical epics? The ones that come out every year around Christmas. Oscar bait. Every single scene is about the big historical prob- lem. Every single conversation is about Hitler or the trenches or the assassination of JFK. I used to like them, before, but after—after, I realized that in real life, no matter what"—she shook her head—"people get up in the morning and they wash their faces and they make themselves breakfast. They tell jokes and they read to their kids and they go on dates and they fall in love and they fuck and they have to wash the dishes and deal with the electric company. What I'm trying to say is, after I left—I mean it was hard, mostly because I didn't know how to talk about it, how to explain what I'd done, what I felt, what I didn't feel. But every morning I got up and I washed my face and I brushed my teeth and I ate my cereal and I went to the office. I went shopping and to the movies, and out to dinner. I dropped clothes off at the dry cleaner's. On a certain level it's grotesque. How we end up, how we always focus—how self-centered we are, how self-centered life forces us to be. I mean, no matter what, even if you're not, you know, personally in the middle of a war, somewhere, someone—*lots* of someones—*are* in the middle of a war, of a famine. And we ignore it. What I'm trying to say is that you can change everything, anything, as long as you're prepared to deal with the consequences. No—that if you change something, you *will* deal with the consequences, even if you're not prepared to. Because you have to. Because the will to survive—no, not to survive, that's too—it's just the bullshit of life. That always trumps—" She shook her head. "Look, like I said, I don't regret it. In some ways, in many ways, logistically, it was hard. But I don't regret it. I packed a bag. I left a note. I blocked his number and I called a lawyer I knew and I told the lawyer that I wanted all further communication with my soon-to-be ex-husband to go through him, the lawyer. All communication with my soon-to-be ex-child, too. I think about her only occasionally. On her birthday. On Mother's Day. When I'm drunk. And when I think about her, mostly it's with relief. That she gets to hate me. Instead of knowing that I—not that I hate, but that I don't feel anything." The woman swam away from me and swam back. "I'm trying to tell you that I was sure. That I *am* sure. That I did the worst thing a woman can do, even though men—you know, you *must* know, men do this *all* the goddamn *time*.

Fuck a woman and make a child and a few weeks or a few months or a few years later they just, you know, they just wander away, and no one— And I say *can*, but it's not that a woman is allowed to do it because in fact it is *not* allowed. It is specifically forbidden. And for no reason except I knew it was right. And that I don't regret it." She laughed again. "You may think I'm a monster. Many women—many people—would. Most, even. And it's not that I don't care. It's that I don't care *enough*. To behave differently. To feel differently. And what is that but more proof? To be so selfish, now—what is that but more proof of the fact that I shouldn't be a part of my daughter's life? How much easier is it, for her, now, to understand this simple story. How helpful. Her mother was—is—a monster. It's a fairy tale, sure. But on some level, I mean—I can see it. I can use words like *simple* or *helpful* or *fairy tale*. But on some level. It's also true."

We were silent for a long while. And then the woman said, "I'm going home." Perhaps I began to say something. Hard to know because before the words could properly form, I saw pale skin flash: the sole of her foot, the back of her hand. She was swimming to shore.

I did not, in fact, think she was a monster. Or, rather, I was not thinking of her, as she swam to shore, at all. I was thinking, as all people who are honest with themselves know they do, after an intimate revelation of this kind, of myself. Of how this reflected on me. I was thinking about the last time I had been as sure of a decision as she had been of hers. Of a decision other than *Yes, in fact I will have this next drink*. I thought about the day I drove to San Francisco. I thought about checking into a hotel there, about sitting down at another hotel's bar. I thought about fucking a stranger and I thought about finding out that I was pregnant by that stranger, and I thought about deciding to keep the child. And I thought, for a long time, of how being in the water, there were so few decisions to make. All of them, in fact—swim left or swim right; swim in or swim out—circling the single, central decision: keep swimming or stop. I paddled for a while, pondering this. Pondering also how tired I was. Of the discrete—as in distinct, as in finite—pleasure I might take in making one last decision and then no more. But I am, as I have said, a practical woman. Which is to say that the pleasures others take in the extremes of both indulgence and renunciation, these luxuries I have never quite been able—though *damn* I was trying—to access. I swam out and I swam out and I swam out, and just before I knew I would be too tired to swim back in, I swam back in. My wallet and my cell phone were gone, but my clothes and my keys, which I'd plunged beneath a mound of sand, were still there. I walked to my car. The sun was coming up. I felt sure I was sober enough to drive.

Los Angeles, 2017

My mother and I were in her kitchen and she was fixing herself a gin and tonic. Four ice cubes in a highball glass, pouring gin for one count, two counts, two and a half. Pouring tonic for one count. More of a splash. I watched her slice a lime, squeeze a wedge over the glass. The windows above her sink, the windows before which she stood, faced west. Saturday, three o'clock, the sun falling to meet the ocean. What filtered in through the windows: light cut with smog, the result the color of Macallan single malt, neat. The glass I was turning in tight circles on the table held nothing stronger than lemonade, but these were still the comparisons that compelled me: sky the color of scotch; bark the syrup-brown of bourbon; cheeks the raw pink of summer's first rosé. I'd driven down for lunch, which she and I had eaten. I had made conversation and refused several plants. Soon I would drive back up.

"So," my mother said, "have you thought about starting to—"

"Mom."

"Honey, there's no need to snap at me."

"I didn't snap."

"And you didn't even let me finish, you don't even know—"

"I do know."

"Well. It's been five years," she said.

"So?"

"So, don't you think it's time to, you know"—she turned and smiled—"get back out there?"

"Mom."

"I ran into—do you remember Barb from book club? Because I had lunch with her at the Americana last Saturday, and it turns out her son is in L.A. now—you remember he was back East for a while after college, working in—advertising I think it was? Well then he decided he wanted to be a doctor so first he had to get a postbac and then there were four years of medical school and—anyway: he just finished his residency at USC—or maybe it was UCLA?—obstetrics I think, obstetrics and gynecology, and of course Barb asked about you and I was telling her, you know, this and that, and then she asked about—"

"Are you trying to set me up with a male gynecologist?"

"Honey, really, there's no need to take that tone with me, I don't see—"

"You don't see what's wrong with male gynecologists."

"No, honey, honestly I don't. But he's not the point, of course you don't have to date *him*, though I did get his number in case—"

"I don't even live in L.A. This is that William Morris job all over—" Do I need to mention that I did not get that job? I did not get that job.

"The *point* is I don't see what's wrong with encouraging you to date." Backlit, my mother was a silhouette in motion, her hips narrow, the edges of her—cheekbones, collarbones, hips, elbows—high and sharp and rapid. You'd have to get closer to see how puffy the skin was under her eyes, how rosy the nose.

"Nothing, Mom. Nothing's wrong with encouraging me to date. And nothing's wrong with me not wanting to." This was not exactly true. Not that there was something wrong with me not wanting to date, just that I did want to.

"Look, I know what you're going through."

"Do you." Only there was a problem.

"You know I was married once, before I met your father." My mother was nodding vigorously and pulling out a chair and settling in at the table for a nice long chat.

A problem that was preventing me from dating.

"Well. After that marriage ended of course it took me forever to, well, get back on the old horse, so to speak"—my mother was, I believe, winking—"so long in fact that I went into therapy to figure out what was wrong with me, if I was blocked or, I don't

know"—in a sort of whisper—"*frigid* or something."
For the record, I don't believe in meditation. I don't
believe in crystals or cleanses or cosmic dusts.

"Was there?" I do believe in playing dead.

"Was there what?"

"Was there something wrong with you?" Playing
dead was what I was doing in this conversation with
my mother. Also what I was doing with respect to
dating.

My mother laughed and took a sip of her gin and
tonic and beaked her head in my direction, her neck
extending confidentially. "Of course not! And even if
there *had* been they never would have told—the point
isn't *blame*, it's *understanding*, it's self-*knowledge*, you
know that, you've been in therapy, haven't you?"

"Okay, so"—trying to work with her—"what did
you learn about yourself?"

"Well first we had to talk about my childhood,
which, you can imagine how long that took, and
then for a while he just asked me about my dreams,
told me to keep a dream journal, made me read him
the entries—he was a Freudian, and Freudians are big
into dreams—so even though I was going three times
a week it was actually *months* before we even started
talking in any really *direct* way about dating—or, well,
about sex. Because that was the problem, really, it
wasn't that I didn't want to date. Or, see, that's what
I figured *out*, it wasn't dating I was afraid of it was
the exposure, the *emotional* exposure of sex. That's

185

what I was worried about. Which actually made a lot of sense because I *loved* flirting"—that flutter of eyelashes again—"and of course it didn't hurt that I was great at it, bantering, that back-and-forth"—is it possible that at some point my mother was capable of listening—"and I loved going to bars with my girlfriends, giving a guy my number, only after—after, when he called, I could never quite say yes to dinner, to drinks, I was just terrified of what would happen. And it wasn't just—it turned out it wasn't just my first marriage, the fact that I'd married so young and trusted my first husband so completely and been—"

"So he was helpful?" Not helpful: the reminder this monologue is furnishing. The reminder of the fact that my mother and I, surface presentation, ability to recognize one's own drinking problem, these things aside, my mother and I, we're quite similar.

"Oh enormously." That she went to a Freudian, this makes sense. Put my dating problem, temporarily, to the side. Know about my mother that she doesn't think much of the middle ground. Very little imagination, great follow-through. "Though not *quite* in the way you might think." She drained her gin and tonic and stood, went to the counter to fix herself another, shot me, on the way, a sly grin. I knew what I should do. I knew I should sit quietly and sip my lemonade and hope my mother's pride prevented her from going on. But fine, I'll admit it. I was curious.

"All right, Mom." She was back at the table now, and she'd found a straw for her drink, metal, congratulations, Mom. "All right, I'll bite. How did he help you?"

"Well." With the metal straw my mother was working quickly. Already a third of her drink had disappeared. "The thing is. So in Freudian therapy you lay on a couch and the therapist sits behind you. I think he explained to me, early on, the point of the tradition, though I can't quite remember now—and anyway, I liked it, not looking at him while he listened to me, it meant I wasn't also trying to figure out what he was thinking of me, trying to read his facial expressions; it can be, you know, very inhibiting."

"I'm sure." My face quiet, eyes blinking.

"But so what this also meant was that I only saw him twice the whole session, once when I came in and then again when I left. So for the whole hour, well, for the whole fifty minutes, he was watching me. It was"—there was an inch of liquid left in her glass, less—"well, frankly it was—"

"Mom, you don't have to—"

"What? It was erotic. You asked." She rolled her eyes, finished her drink, got up to fix herself a third. "This was"—her back was to me now—"right around the time your grandmother got sick. And then when she died, well, without her working there was no more money for extravagances, and your grandfather considered therapy—analysis—an extravagance.

So I told Robert—Rob—my analyst, I told him I would have to stop going to therapy. To analysis. He offered me a reduced rate, but I was barely working, picking up boom work on little films here and there, even at the fee he was suggesting, I just couldn't afford it. Did I tell you—I didn't, I should"—her head whipped around, her eyes, could they possibly have been twinkling—"how attractive he was? Square jaw, broad shoulders, thick, black hair, a mustache, I thought maybe he'd been in the army, gone to grad school on the GI bill, though I guess he could have just been"—she shrugged, turned back to her drink, squeezed a wedge of lime, carried the glass back to the table—"I mean it was all pretty standard issue, but it was his looks—how different he looked from what I assumed a therapist, an analyst, would look like, back then I thought all Freudians looked like, well, Freud, a thousand years old and pipe-smoking and bearded—plus the watching, how I'd held, sure, for a fee, but how I'd held his attention. And the fact that it was wrong, of course that helped, plus the power he had, I mean the power he had over me. He already knew all my secrets, the things you keep from boyfriends at first, and besides I knew he liked me, a woman always does, which always makes a man more attractive. So our last session, I get up off the couch, I turn around, and we shake hands, and he holds my hand maybe a second too long. And I look up at him and I ask him if we can, now that,

you know, he's no longer my therapist, my analyst"—
she twirled the ice in her glass with the straw, took a
long sip—"I ask him whether I can take him out for
a drink. And he says no. Well, at first he says no. He
puts his hands in his pockets and he says that while
yes, of course he'd love to, he can't. It just wouldn't
be—he says something about medical ethics. But
I'm—you know at this point I'm twenty-three, and
I have these long legs and I'm wearing a dress that's
maybe a little too low—"

"Mom."

"What, I was wearing a low-cut dress, what's wrong
with that?" Another long sip. "And I say, I ask him if
he couldn't make, just this once, an exception."

"You slept with him didn't you."

"Right there, on the couch. He missed his next
appointment."

"You're—"

"Of course I'm kidding." My mother's tone was
highest dudgeon. "Though honestly the fact that
you might have thought we actually *did*—I mean
what do you *think* of me, that you think I would—"

"But you did sleep with him."

My mother smiled. "So, I ask him if he would
consider, just this once, making an exception, and
he, well, he makes this face, this face like he wants to
say yes but he knows he shouldn't and I take a step
in and my breasts are just"—she drew out the word
just, enjoying herself—"brushing the lapels of his suit

189

jacket, and I say, One drink, and he says, Okay, one drink."

"You slept with him."

"I slept with him." The smile triumphant. "And it was—I thought it then and I think it now. It was very therapeutic. One of the most helpful things about therapy, or analysis—they say one of the most helpful things is how the therapeutic relationship mirrors relationships in the real world, only it has these boundaries, in other words it's kind of a"—her fingers sketched canted quotes—"safe space."

"But he violated those boundaries."

"No, *I* violated those boundaries. And it proved a larger point, that I could be totally emotionally open with someone, totally vulnerable, and he would still want to sleep with me."

"I hope you reported him."

"Of course I didn't report him, god, you're such a prude." My mother rolled her eyes. "I mean it was my idea to—"

"And it was his responsibility."

"The point is it worked. We went out for a drink and he took me back to his apartment and after that"—my mother's hand sliced the air—"just like that. Cured. I was cured. I met your father a week later, and I would *never* have been open to him if I hadn't had this experience with Rob, so whatever you think of it, you should also"—another long sip and her third gin and tonic was gone—"be grateful I

190

did because if I hadn't I would never have dated your father and if I hadn't dated your father, well, where would *you* be?" My mother stood. "Whether or not you believe it was *appropriate,* whether or not you think it *helped*—the point is *I* think it helped. And if I think it helped, well then"—she waved the hand that wasn't holding the glass—"it did. If only because I *believe* it did."

My mother and father are still together. Point for the analyst, I suppose. They live together in a house, in the very house in whose kitchen I was then sitting. Occasionally, they can still be glimpsed passing, both of them, through the same room at the same time. Say it's the living room: she likely heading to the kitchen, he likely to his studio. The studio is where my father spends most of his time. He paints. On commission mostly: cheerful seaside scenes; the portraits my parents' richer friends request of their trust-funded daughters. He was, I'm almost certain, painting one of those daughters while my mother and I talked. For the record, my parents are very much in love. No one, for example, has ever seen them fight. Often they attend parties together. My father knows how to make my mother a perfect gin martini, is in fact the only one allowed to mix them for her, she doesn't even trust herself. So then does it matter that my mother's father, long dead, was a cinematographer, by his own account very talented, so talented he wouldn't deign to work on any but the very best pictures. The very best pictures: over the course of forty years, a total of six came his way. Does it matter that even the most predatory therapist, analyst, could see, in my mother's choice of husband, an artist who welcomes compromise, a rejection of her father, an artist who refused it? That he, my father, makes, regardless, not nearly enough money? That my mother met my father when she agreed to be a live model for the figure-drawing class he was teaching at a community college? Nude live model, I should say. Her long legs, the breasts she showed off in that low-cut dress, here, too, they served her well.

But the dating problem. My mother, it should by now be clear, chooses men poorly, and so do I, and this is why I was not dating, do not date. What was happening to me then, at the time when I sat in my mother's kitchen and turned my sweating glass of lemonade on a damp coaster, was not unlike the problem that had driven my mother to analysis, to her analyst. I've said that I did want to date and that there was a problem preventing me, but this, too, is not quite accurate. The truth is I wanted to date and for a time I did, I went on dates with lovely men, men with advanced degrees and wit to spare and working definitions of the word *feminism* and shoulders just as broad as my mother's GI turned analyst. And when they bent down to kiss me my entire body recoiled. Their lips fell on mine and it was as if every cell in my body began immediately trying to pull away. I could feel my pores shrink, the little hairs on my arms retract, anything my body could do to put even a negligible, an imaginary distance between itself, between myself, and these men. I mean, anything besides actually pulling away. Meanwhile at work, alone in an office with the oldest, the sweatiest, the baldest of our lawyers, I found myself blushing, found my knees growing weak, found myself backing toward the door, trying again to put as much distance between me and the decaying specimen before me—but this time it was to stop myself from jumping him. It was like I was being reminded that I *could* feel desire. But then also that desire was purposely being misdirected so that I wouldn't have sex. And I didn't know what to do with that. With my body telling me, You don't want to fuck these men that you are—that you *should* be—attracted to. With my body telling me, You *do* want to fuck this eighty-five-year old lawyer who thinks corporations should have the same rights as individuals and whose youngest granddaughter is just about your age. I didn't know what to do with my body telling me *You don't want what you want.*

My mother walked to the counter and made herself a fourth gin and tonic. I watched her drink it. Our talk became small. Before I left, I washed my own glass out, filled another with water, put it on the table like a suggestion.

San Joaquin Valley, 2017

I left my mother's house and I drove home. The town in which I live is far from the coast, the water, salt spray, beauty. What it is close to: the 5, a cattle ranch, a state prison, a mental hospital. The law firm where I am a legal secretary is in downtown Fresno and on weekdays I commute, an hour in every morning, an hour back every night. Often I am asked why I have chosen to live so far from my place of employment. Usually I plead poverty and when I do I am believed, though Fresno is by no means a desirable place in which to live and there are affordable neighborhoods much closer to its center. Still, it's hard to argue with a single mother, what with the cost of childcare, the cost of kids. Sometimes I say nothing. Silence: the great conversation killer. In truth I moved to this town because in the months immediately before I stopped drinking I was drinking a great deal and sleeping very little. My son, by this time a toddler, was plagued by nightmares, woke crying almost every night, so that my own sleep was only ever partial, alert as I felt I had to be to my son's bleats of distress. I became eventually so attuned to the sound of his breath growing faster and more shallow, to the quickening rustle of his bedsheets, to the soft mewling that presaged a full-throated shout, that I often arrived at his bedside a moment before he opened his mouth to scream. And because I was not always as quiet as I intended to be, moving from my room to his, it was sometimes the case that when I arrived at his bedside I found him sitting up, eyes open, asking me if he had had another night-mare, which he pronounced *no-more,* which, at least partially intoxicated as I always was, I found heart-breaking in its *just so*–ness. And because, though I had not heard his screams, I felt certain that, had he not heard my feet against the wood of the hallway that connected my room to his, he would neverthe-less have woken himself up with his cries, I always said yes; with tears in my eyes at how small he was, at how dear he was, at how vulnerable, I said yes and, saying yes, would take him in my arms and bring him to my bed, where he would drift off, his head on my lap, me sitting up, my back against the wall, my hand lifting a low glass ever emptier of bourbon from my bedside table to my mouth until my alarm went off and it was time to get up.

It was during these hours, between midnight and morning, in the space between waking and sleep-ing, between sober and drunk, that I remembered a short story I'd once read. The author was male. Male and from California and a playwright as well as a writer of short stories, and sometimes also a painter, also an actor, also a singer of country-and-western songs. Exemplary jeans-wearer. All these facts of the essence. My son and I were, at this point, living in an apartment in the city in which I worked. Before that we'd lived in Los Angeles, on the first floor of a two-story several blocks from my parents' house, the two-story owned by friends of my parents, my parents also paying the majority of the greatly reduced rent. But then I got the job in Fresno, two hundred or so miles north of Los Angeles, and I moved, this move financed by my parents, the rent of the apartment, too spacious, to which my son and I moved, subsidized, as the rent in Los Angeles had been, by my parents. They worried about me, hadn't wanted me to move away, agreed only, in the end, if I let them pay most of the rent so I'd have plenty of money left over for the gas that would be required for frequent trips down south, to visit them, in the used car they had also paid for. In part I drank to forget the fact of their charity. Charity that they could ill afford. On the night I remembered the jeans-wearer's short story, my divorce, dragged out far longer than necessary by John's groundless hope that we might reconcile, had recently been finalized. Or else was about to be. And in any case I'd heard from my lawyer, whom my parents had hired and whom they were of course also paying, that because California was a community-property state, I could theoretically be entitled not only to alimony but also to half of John's assets. I waived alimony, waived any claims to his income, his savings, his 401(k), but John, newly flush—he'd just received a modest inheritance from a generous aunt who had died before we'd divorced but whose will had only recently been probated—insisted I take a lump sum in cash. For the baby, he said. He was, as I've said—he is—a very kind man. The dollar amount was hardly extravagant, four figures after taxes, but it would, I suspected, be enough for a down payment on a house in the town mentioned in the short story I'd read.

There was a town in the short story. I should have mentioned that earlier. There was a town in the short story. Or there were towns, many of them. In the story, a man leaves his wife. He drives down the Maine coast. He reaches a town. He calls another woman from a pay phone. He tells her that he's left his wife to be with her. She tells him she won't leave her husband. He hangs up. He gets back in his car. Not his car. His truck. He keeps driving. There is a second town. The pattern repeats itself. In each town, there is a different woman. Each woman, despite the promises it is implied she has made, refuses to leave her husband. He drives down the Eastern Seaboard. He drives across the South. He drives up through the Plains states and west through the Rockies. In each town he is rejected. He does not stop to sleep or to eat or to take a shit, or if he does, the jeans-wearing author will not speak of it. At last he lands in a town in California. The town whose name I now, drinking, dozing, remembered. He makes a call, finds that the number has been disconnected. The story ends there, but I always imagined him staying. How can he leave? He has run out of road.

The reader senses that the man's promiscuity, his faithlessness, is to blame for his being repeatedly rejected. But this sense is overridden, and deliberately, by the anger the reader also feels toward the women he has called. He has driven so far. He's been driving for days. Can one of these women not offer him a meal, a bed, the comforts of her flesh, if only for one night? I read once that violence onscreen, even if it is designed to appall, argues, inevitably, for itself. That the viewer is always inherently intrigued and therefore aroused by it. That the visual fact of violence is titillating, even if the intent is to disgust. And so one feels not disgust but pity for the lone driver. The writer who depicts an abhorrent male character still demands that the reader pay the abhorrent man his attention.

Did I imagine myself as the lone driver, making a life for myself in a town full of strangers? Yes I did. Pay attention to enough men and you will begin to think of yourself as one. You will think of this as an improvement over fantasizing about being mistreated by one and you will, probably, be right. I mean, also the bourbon helped. So I put a down payment on a house and my son and I moved out of the apartment in Fresno and into the house I had bought and then, sometime after, I quit drinking, a process that involved dropping my son off at my parents' house and checking myself into a rehab facility my parents had paid for and my parents also, for a time, paying the mortgage on the house I had bought, so that when I left rehab, though I refused to attend meetings of any kind, found the idea of sharing, of a higher power, of making amends, repulsive, I nevertheless remained sober because I had discovered it was the only way I could prevent my parents from helping me financially in any way. By *prevent* I mean *avoid the necessity of.* Pride kept me sober. Also anger, also stubbornness. Worth mentioning, too, that getting sober also helped me realize the mistake I had made, looking at a dusty, deserted, racially segregated, economically deprived town and seeing *quaint,* and here, too, it was pride and anger and stubbornness that kept me from admitting I'd been very drunk and very wrong, pride and anger and stubbornness that kept me from selling the house. Also, realistically, no one would have bought it. With the minuscule down payment that I had scraped together, no surprise that the place was a dump.

———

When I reached the home I am still now, without my parents' help, paying off, only one light was on. I had made improvements to the house since purchasing it, since sobering up, but this is not the kind of narrative in which I now detail those improvements and extol the redemptive power of physical labor, though I do in fact believe in said redemptive power, as I believe in the redemptive power of almost anything that is unpleasant and/or difficult. Anyway. Just, the house was nicer. That's the important part.

It was nine o'clock and my son had been, if the sitter had followed my instructions, which she always does, asleep for an hour. The sitter is my age, a fact about which I feel some guilt. Or, she is the age I still usually imagine myself to be. In fact she is roughly a decade younger. She dropped out of college to care for her parents, who contracted, within the span of several months, two different but equally rare cancers. When chemo and radiation failed, when it became clear that surgery would do more harm than good, she came home and set them up in twin hospital beds in the living room of her childhood home and cared for them. Sometimes she tells me stories about the last few months of their lives, stories I enjoy not because they are affecting but because they are gruesome. Not affecting, well, not affecting for me.

When I entered my house, the sitter was on the couch, looking at her phone.

"Hey," I said.

"Oh." She turned. "Hey, you're back. How's your mom?"

"Fine. How were things here?"

She shrugged. "Fine. Had a little trouble getting him to bed. He wanted a second story, and then a third." She rolled her eyes, smiled. "Nothing unusual."

"Well," I said. "Thank you." I paused. "I know he really likes you," I said. Though she had been my sitter at this point already for many months, and though she had told me about rubbing lotion into the cracked skin of her father's feet, cutting his hard and yellowed toenails, holding her mother over the toilet and wiping her ass, running a sponge under her arms and between her legs, I still felt, still feel, in her presence, a profound awkwardness. As if she might at any moment decide—not to quit but to humiliate me. I don't keep a journal but I sometimes felt, sometimes feel, in her presence, as if I do, and have forgotten, and that she's read it, and is about to post its contents on her blog. This is my standard reaction to the fact of a slowly growing—as opposed to an immediate and overwhelming—intimacy. My therapist—I don't work the steps, but I lost the argument with myself on therapy—says understanding the problem is the first step to fixing it and I agree, only I'm not sure whether I care to take any further action. And yes I know no one keeps blogs anymore.

———

The babysitter and I talked for a while, first about my mother and then about hers, about her mother's depression, untreated, and it occurred to me, and not for the first time, that in addition to the anxiety I experience when threatened with intimacy per se, in the babysitter's case the fear that her past seemed likely to be my future—my parents are aging; I am an only child; there is no money for nursing homes— might also be a contributing factor. My therapist would have wanted me to share this fear, would have urged me to in this way make myself vulnerable, might even have suggested that I ask the babysitter about the fears she herself had experienced when she'd learned of her parents' diagnoses, when she'd understood that the next months, the next years of her life would have to be devoted to caring for them. But I was not then, am not now, so evolved. I asked my babysitter how much I owed her and I wrote her a check and I said, as she shouldered her backpack and moved toward the door, "See you Monday."

After she left I looked at my phone for a while. By *looked* I mean *stared,* stared specifically at the phone number I wasn't entirely sure was still Laura's. Two visits ago my mother had mentioned that Laura had stopped by, that she was pregnant, that her third husband seemed like a keeper, a little younger than her, devoted, doted on her, which sounded nice enough for Laura, not everyone is as immediately repulsed by tenderness as I am. It was the fact that she was pregnant, it created what a more optimistic woman might have called possibility. All my friends—all the people I knew by name and saw on purpose more than twice a month—were moms. Laura was going to be a mom. Perhaps she could, by the transitive property of moms really having very few options when it came to socializing, again be my friend. My own mother had offered to give me Laura's number, and I had said, No, thanks, I already have it, and since then I had been staring at the number, on and off, and wondering whether in fact I did and, if I did, whether I should do something about it.

Maybe five minutes of staring, of turning the phone's screen on and off, of not calling, and then I checked on my son. Sober I walk more softly and he was asleep when I opened the door and still asleep as I approached his bed and leaned over his supine body and kissed him on the forehead. In the living room I turned on the TV. I checked my phone. When I worry about my son of course I worry about him dying, but when I have convinced myself that he is still breathing, that his pupils do not look jaundiced, that the lump that forms on his forehead when he bumps his head cannot also be concealing a tumor, what I worry about is how he'll end up. I mean the possibility that he'll end up like me. Not that I'm so horrible, just that I know I can do a great, an excellent, a perfect—I mean, my parents were *fine*. They weren't amazing but certainly they did not encourage me to hate myself. They did not tell me to seek out men who were controlling and cruel, they did not suggest this is what I deserved. And if there was, during my formative years, a certain cultural consensus about what women wanted and how men should go about giving it to them, well, many others of my generation were smart enough to be skeptical of it. What I'm saying is that my life, like the lives of most people, lacks an origin story. I mean one with any explanatory power. Which means that my son could turn out any way and for any reason or for no reason at all. I'm not sure if it's irony but here it is, at last I've found the thing I do want to control, and of course I can't.

When I bought the house I did so in part because I had a romantic notion about the turn my life might take in such a town, so small and dead-ended. I imagined myself working at a diner, a diner frequented by truckers. I imagined one of them, kindhearted, modifying his routes so he could see me more often. Never staying longer than the time it took to drink two cups of coffee and eat a grilled cheese, but nevertheless, an understanding growing between us. I imagined myself in a long dress, in a backyard, hanging my sheets out to dry on a clothesline. Shielding my eyes from the sun. Instead I pay a woman to care for my son while I work as a legal secretary. All my skirts hit just below the knee. To clean these clothes, I use a washing machine and a dryer, both located in the basement. In the short story I read, the protagonist has a son, a son whom he leaves, with his wife, on the Eastern Seaboard. The author, the jeans-wearer, had a number of children. They are scattered about the country with the women who bore them. And though yes, it is true that the author never got sober, perhaps all this time I have been wrong about the story's protagonist, the man who runs out of road. Because he hasn't, not really. I mean, he can drive into the ocean. He can always decide to turn around.

WORKS (NOT) CITED

This manuscript emerged in part from an engagement with and in some cases refers elliptically to the following texts, television shows, films, web series, works of art, songs, e-mail newsletters, and podcasts: *Speedboat* and *Pitch Dark*, Renata Adler; *Phantom Thread*, written and directed by Paul Thomas Anderson; *Hotel Chevalier*, directed by Wes Anderson; *Unmastered*, Katherine Angel; *Frasier*, Seasons 1–11, created by David Angell, Peter Casey, and David Lee; *Fish Tank*, directed by Andrea Arnold; *Clouds of Sils Maria* and *Personal Shopper*, directed by Olivier Assayas; *All Grown Up*, Jami Attenberg; *Rocky*, directed by John G. Avildsen; *John*, Annie Baker; *Cassandra at the Wedding*, Dorothy Baker; *Giovanni's Room*, James Baldwin; *The Big Blue*, directed by Luc Besson; *Out of This World*, created by John Boni and Bob Booker; *Horace and Pete*, written and directed by Louis C.K., especially Episode 3, starring Laurie Metcalf; *The Years of Lyndon Johnson*, Robert Caro; "The Glass Essay," Anne Carson; "Fresno's Ugly Divide," a multi-part series published by *The Atlantic* and written by Rachel Cassandra, Misyrlena Egkolfopoulou, Briana Flin, Alexandria Fuller, Margaret Katcher, Mary Newman, and Reis Thebault, graduate students at U.C. Berkeley's

Graduate School of Journalism; *Husbands* and *Minnie and Moskowitz*, written and directed by John Cassavetes; *The Handmaiden*, directed by Park Chan-wook; *Mrs. Bridge*, Evan S. Connell; "Reading the Tarot," an e-mail newsletter written by Jessa Crispin; *In the Last Analysis*, Amanda Cross; *Outline* and *Transit*, Rachel Cusk; the e-mail newsletter associated with "The Small Bow," a website created by A. J. Daulerio and illustrated by Edith Zimmerman; "Shitty Media Men," a crowdsourced Google spreadsheet created by Moira Donegan; *The Possession*, Annie Ernaux (trans. Anna Moschovakis); reporting in *The New Yorker* on Harvey Weinstein by Ronan Farrow; *Veronica*, Mary Gaitskill; *The Babysitter at Rest*, Jen George; *The End of the Novel of Love*, Vivian Gornick; *Call Me by Your Name*, directed by Luca Guadagnino; *I Love Dick*, created by Sarah Gubbins and Jill Soloway, especially Episode 5, "A Short History of Weird Girls," written by Annie Baker, Chris Kraus, and Heidi Schreck; *The Piano Teacher*, directed by Michael Haneke; *L.A. Confidential*, directed by Curtis Hanson; *Writing a Woman's Life*, Carolyn G. Heilbrun; "Invictus," William Ernest Henley; *How Should a Person Be?*, Sheila Heti; "The Oppositional Gaze: Black Female Spectators," bell hooks; *Three Times*, directed by Hou Hsiao-hsien; *In a Lonely Place*, Dorothy B. Hughes; *Negroland*, Margo Jefferson; *Moonstruck*, directed by Norman Jewison; *The Folded Clock*, Heidi Julavits; *The First Bad Man*, Miranda July; reporting in *The New York Times* about workplace sexual harassment led by Jodi Kantor and Megan

Twohey; *Big Little Lies*, created by David E. Kelley; *I Love Dick*, Chris Kraus; *The Journals of Sylvia Plath 1950–1962*, edited by Karen V. Kukil; *Suite for Barbara Loden*, Nathalie Léger; *August: Osage County*, Tracy Letts; *The Widening Spell of the Leaves*, Larry Levis; *Margaret*, directed by Kenneth Lonergan; *Her Body and Other Parties*, Carmen Maria Machado; *Shame*, directed by Steve McQueen; *The Collected Stories*, Leonard Michaels; *The Journalist and the Murderer*, Janet Malcolm; *The English Patient*, directed by Anthony Minghella; "Visual Pleasure and Narrative Cinema," Laura Mulvey; *Blank Check with Griffin and David*, hosted by Griffin Newman and David Sims, especially the December 23, 2018, episode on *Aquaman*, directed by James Wan; *And Now We Have Everything*, Meaghan O'Connell; *The English Patient*, Michael Ondaatje; *New Collected Poems*, George Oppen; *Meaning a Life*, Mary Oppen; *Where Should We Begin?*, Season 1, hosted by Esther Perel; *Parallel Lives*, Phyllis Rose; *Mating*, Norman Rush; "Reading Women's Lives," compiled by Professor Georganne Schriner, Arizona State University; *Goodfellas* and *Casino*, directed by Martin Scorsese; *The Rings of Saturn*, W. G. Sebald; "Push," written by Matt Serletic and Rob Thomas, performed by Matchbox Twenty; *Secretary*, directed by Steven Shainberg; *The West Wing*, Seasons 1–3, created by Aaron Sorkin; "Does Anyone Have the Right to Sex?" Amia Srinivasan, *London Review of Books*, Vol 40, No. 6, March 22, 2018; *Want* and *When the Saints*, Lynn Steger Strong; *Antígona González*, Sara Uribe (trans. John Pluecker); *Jane the Virgin*, created by

Jennie Snyder Urman; "On Pandering," an essay by Claire Vaye Watkins given as a lecture during the 2015 Tin House Summer Workshop and reprinted in the 2015 Winter Issue of *Tin House* magazine; *Basic Instinct*, directed by Paul Verhoeven; *Fleabag*, created by Phoebe Waller-Bridge; "Ventimiglia," Joanna Walsh; *Mad Men*, Seasons 6–7, created by Matthew Weiner, especially Season 6, Episode 7, "Man with a Plan," starring Linda Cardellini; *Drive*, directed by Nicolas Winding Refn; "Burn This," Lanford Wilson; *Heroines*, Kate Zambreno; *Sour Heart*, Jenny Zhang.

WORKS CITED

The line "Happy, with a secret," quoted by the tenant in "Ann Arbor, 2002," is spoken by Mark Ruffalo's character, Stan, in *Eternal Sunshine of the Spotless Mind*, directed by Michel Gondry. Though the film premiered in 2004 and so could not have been seen by the tenant at the time she "quotes" it, the reference is deliberate.

The Swedish video artist's exhibit described in "San Francisco, 2010," was, in part, inspired by Sophie Calle's *Missing*, an exhibition on view at San Francisco's Fort Mason Center for Arts & Culture from June 29 to August 20, 2017.

The details of the party at which Norman Mailer stabbed his second wife, née Adele Morales, and of his relationship with her, is drawn from various texts including *Mailer: A Biography*, by Mary V. Dearborn; *Norman Mailer: The American*, directed by Joseph Mantegna; and *The Last Party: Scenes from My Life with Norman Mailer*, by Adele Mailer.

The short story described by the narrator in "San Joaquin Valley, 2017," is inspired by Sam Shephard's short story, "Coalinga ½ Way."

Works Cited

Also in "San Joaquin Valley, 2017," the text the narrator refers to but cannot remember and which proposes that violence onscreen argues, inevitably, for itself, is Renata Adler's "...The Movies Make Heroes of Them All," an essay collected in *A Year in the Dark*.

The idea of a "Works (Not) Cited" section comes from Azareen Van der Vliet Oloomi's novel *Fra Keeler*.

ACKNOWLEDGMENTS

A writer shoves into her first novel more or less everything she has ever thought, seen, read, loved, hated, experienced. I believe this, true or false. Put another way: I have done this, good or bad. What I mean to say is that if I were to acknowledge every single person, institution, or text that supported or inspired me during the gestation of or found its way somehow into *Topics of Conversation*, this section would be longer than the novel itself. What I mean also to say is: if we've ever had a conversation or shared a meal or even traded work e-mails, thank you.

Thank you to my parents, Ada and Michael. Thank you to the Popkeys: Dan and Nick and Challis; Ross and Kristi; Sally and Kent. Thank you to the Marcheses: Giuseppina and Salvatore; Antonella and Paolo; Anna and Claudio and Gaetano and Jessica and Davide; Mina and Luca and Caterina and Aurora. Thank you to the MacLaughlins: Ann; Jay; Nina; Sam; and Molly Fischer and Pam Murray.

In St. Louis, thank you to Washington University and to the writers in the fiction cohorts above and below mine: Sara Duff and Jae Kim and Meghan Lamb and Joel

Sherman and Paul Sung; Elizabeth Baird and Rebecca Butler and Charles McCrory and Madeleine Moss and Analeah Rosen and Red Samaniego. Special thanks to the fiction writers in my cohort: Miguel Morales and Erin Peraza and Robin Tripp and Jenny Wu. Thank you to Cassie Donish and again Sara Duff and Erinrose Mager and Emma Wilson and Sasha Wiseman and Christina Wood Martinez and Billy Youngblood. Thank you to my professors: Kathryn Davis and Danielle Dutton and Marshall Klimasewiski; also Steven Meyer and Martin Riker. Thank you to Shannon Rabong and to Dave Schuman.

Thank you to Julia Galeota. Thank you to Emily Gould, Lynn Steger Strong, and Monika Woods.

Thank you to my therapist in New York and my therapist in St. Louis, neither of whom I have slept with.

Thank you to 67 Edgewood and the QuikTrip on Kingshighway and the fried chicken at Schnucks.

Thank you to Louise Glück, who gave me permission to write fiction.

Thank you to Ben Marcus, who gave me permission to write a novel.

Thank you to Denise Shannon and Jordan Pavlin for placing their trust in me as a writer and in this manuscript as a book before I had much of any in either. Thank you to Jacqueline Sather and Nicholas Thomson. At Knopf, thank you to the production editor, Andrew Dorko; the managing editor, Kathy Hourigan; the production manager, Lorraine Hyland; the text designer, Anna Knighton; Emily Murphy in marketing; Emily Reardon in publicity; and the copyeditor, Bonnie Thompson. Thank you to Maria Švarbová, whose stunning photograph is used on the jacket; thank you to Jennifer Carrow and Sinem Erkas for their work on the jacket. Thank you to Brian Etling in sales. At Serpent's Tail, thank you to Peter Dyer, the creative director; Graeme Hall, the editorial manager; Ali Nadal, the production manager; Hannah Ross, the publicity director; and especially Nick Sheerin, the acquiring editor. Thank you to Debra Helfand, for teaching me the value of a good managing editor.

Thank you to Gabriel Winslow-Yost for his friendship and for innumerable book and film recommendations and most especially for suffering through an early draft of this novel, even the icky sex bits.

Thank you to Zan Romanoff and Nozlee Samadzadeh-Hadidi for loving me even and especially when I insist I do not wish to be loved.

Thank you to Dudley, aka the Hund, aka Hundable, aka the Hundable Notion, aka the Notional Concept, aka Meefy. You are not a very good editor, but you are a very good dog.

And thank you to Will. All we need is just a little patience.